CW01499462

ACKNOWLEDGMENTS

Thanks to Tod Clark, Donna Fitzpatrick, Paul Goblirsch, Leigh Haig, Lynne Hansen, Xtina Marie, Michael McBride, Jim Morey, Becky Narron, Rhonda Rettig, and Paul Synuria II for their spoooooky help with this novel.

SICK HOUSE

JEFF STRAND

ISBN-13: 978-1985576544
ISBN-10: 1985576546

PROLOGUE

Gina Atherton would never, ever harm a living creature, but that didn't mean she wouldn't play with its bones after it was dead.

She'd covered her dining room table with several layers of newspaper and then set out her collection of skeletons. Two cats, a small dog, a squirrel, a rat, and a snake, along with a deer skull. The rat, snake, and deer bones she'd bought from a taxidermy shop. The cats and squirrel she'd found, mostly intact, by the side of the road; she'd taken them home and let nature do the rest. She couldn't remember how she'd gotten the dog.

Now the fun part. Mix and match. Maybe she'd make a snake with a rat's head. Or a dog with a squirrel's head. Or a deer head with eight cat-legs.

So many possibilities.

Once they were done, Gina would bury them in the flower garden. She smiled at the thought of them being uncovered, whether it was soon after she moved away, or years after she was dead.

Gina was a realist. She knew that the next people who lived in this house were unlikely to shout, "*Oh my God! It's a cat-legged deer-head! What an amazing scientific discovery!*" It was satisfying enough that they'd wonder what kind of deranged person would bury bones like this.

She loved to think that they'd question her sanity.

Her sister wouldn't appreciate this. Her sister didn't like her acting crazy. But Gina didn't have to tell her about the bones, did she?

It amused her to picture somebody lying in bed, staring at the ceiling, thinking *A crazy lady used to live here.* Maybe they'd worry that she'd never left. Not a legitimate worry, of course, but a small nagging one they couldn't quite dismiss...

Though she knew this made her a bad person, it delighted her even more to think of a child needing to be comforted by his or her parents. *"Is the woman who buried the bones still here?"*

"Of course not, honey."

"Is she hiding under my bed?"

"You know she isn't."

"What if she's in my closet?"

"She's not. I promise. Please go to sleep. It's late and you have school tomorrow."

"But I'm scared."

Gina looked at the bones strewn on her table and clapped her hands in glee.

So very many possibilities.

CHAPTER ONE

"Gardner! Get your ass in here!"

Boyd Gardner looked up from the table saw. Mr. Prace was not the kind of boss to grab a beer with his employees after work, but he also wasn't one to abuse his authority. If he was shouting from the other side of the floor, this was serious.

Boyd set down the plywood that he hadn't yet started cutting and removed his safety goggles. The other guys on the floor gave him a variety of looks: sympathy, confusion, and (mostly) relief that it wasn't them getting yelled at.

Mr. Prace gestured. "In my fucking office! Now!"

Cursing, though not unheard of, was rare. He'd certainly never shouted the f-word in front of everyone. As Boyd hurried past the other workstations, he desperately hoped this was some kind of misunderstanding.

Mr. Prace walked into his office and Boyd followed. A man Boyd didn't recognize stood next to Mr. Prace's desk. He was wearing a dress shirt and tie and sure looked like he could be from Human Resources. Boyd felt a little sick to his stomach.

3

"Take off your gloves," said Mr. Prace. "Show some respect."

"Sorry, sir," said Boyd, taking off his work gloves. This was not traditionally a "sir" environment, but it seemed appropriate now.

"Have a seat."

Boyd sat down on one of the two chairs in front of Mr. Prace's small wobbly desk. They made furniture here, so Boyd had never been sure if the desk was an intentional or accidental irony.

Mr. Prace remained standing. He didn't acknowledge the other man in the room. "Boyd, sometimes our past actions come back to haunt us. I want you to think back to a conversation from three months ago."

Boyd had no idea what he was talking about. "I'm not sure what you mean, sir."

"You can stop calling me sir. Being a kiss-ass isn't going to change this. Where were you three months ago?"

Boyd shrugged. "I can't remember."

I can't lose my job. I can't lose my job. I am so deeply screwed if I lose my job.

He'd been working here for four years. Surely he'd just get a severe reprimand for whatever it was, right? Especially since he had no clue what it could possibly be. His attendance had been perfect since the doctors gave his daughter Paige a clean bill of health, and that was a year ago. He was never late. He sure as hell hadn't sexually harassed anyone. Whatever he'd done to screw up three months ago couldn't be a fireable offense.

"You were right here. We were doing your annual performance review."

Boyd nodded. It had gone pretty well. Now he was

even more baffled.

"Do you remember what you said?"

"I...thanked you at the end?"

Mr. Prace folded his arms across his chest. "You said that you were interested in moving up the chain of command. Said you'd like to be a supervisor someday. Well, Boyd, you've got yourself a promotion."

Boyd stared at him, not quite processing what he was hearing.

Mr. Prace grinned. "We're moving you to the Kirkland location. You've now got longer hours, more headaches, and more money. Congratulations."

"Oh my God." Boyd exhaled a sigh of relief. "You almost gave me a heart attack."

"C'mon, you know you do great work. I hate to lose somebody like you, but this is an outstanding opportunity and I'm sure you'll make the best of it. You'd said that you were willing to relocate. That's still true, right?"

Boyd nodded. "Yes, yes. Adeline hates her job. My job is the only thing keeping us here."

Mr. Prace pointed at the man in the tie. "He'll talk to you about the details. We'll be sending you to some training, but I'm sure you'll breeze right through it; I've seen the way you interact with the other guys on the floor."

"Thank you. This means a lot."

"When you're done here, you can either walk out with your head hung and keep the joke going or just tell them the truth. Your call."

"I'll probably just tell them."

"That's fine."

- - -

Though Boyd was not typically a "crank up the music and drum your hands against the steering wheel" kind of guy, this was no ordinary day. It took him a minute to find a radio station that was playing something sufficiently hard rocking, but once he did, he turned the volume up as loud as he could without getting distortion from the old speakers.

There were two pizza boxes on the passenger seat. Pizza was typically a Saturday night treat, but not only was Boyd breaking tradition regarding the day of the week, he'd gone to one of the *good* pizza places. Supervisors didn't have to get their pizza from restaurants that stingily parsed out pepperoni in such a way that two pieces on a single slice was cause for celebration. Tonight, Boyd Gardner's family was having *double* pepperoni. With extra cheese. And garlic butter dipping sauce. No cinnamon sticks, though; those would have to wait until he was established in his new position.

He'd hoped that at thirty-two years old he'd be doing a better job of providing for his family. Not that he was doing a terrible job. After all, they had a roof over their heads, food on the table, and no rats scurried over them while they slept. But they lived in a cramped apartment where his two daughters had to share a room, and where he and Adeline had to listen to the neighbors on the other side of the wall have painful-sounding sex every Thursday night.

Not anymore.

Though it wasn't as if they were suddenly fabulously wealthy monocle-wearing socialites, the lives of the Gardners were about to get a lot better.

- - -

"Daddy!" shouted his eight-year-old daughter Naomi as he walked into the apartment. She allowed him just enough time to place the boxes on the dining room table, then gave him one of her legendary rib-splintering hugs.

Adeline closed her laptop and got up off the couch. "What's this?" she asked.

"Pizza," Boyd informed her.

"I know that, Mr. Obvious, but what's the occasion? Did you rob a pizza place?"

"Nope."

Adeline gave him a suspicious look. "You seem weirdly giddy."

"All will be explained."

"I'll get the paper plates." As Adeline walked into the kitchen, Boyd watched her ass. He didn't look at her ass nearly often enough these days. That was going to change.

It was, after all, an ass that should have been out of his league. Unlike Boyd, Adeline was tall, slender, and pleasing to the eye. Boyd kept in sort of decent shape, but he had a face like an action figure that had melted just a bit. Though he didn't frighten young children, in terms of handsomeness Adeline had not won the husband lottery. ("Good thing you care more about charm than looks," he'd often say. She'd scold him for making fun of his appearance, and also playfully warn him not to overestimate his charm.) He was going prematurely gray, though he didn't think it looked bad, and he had a lot more lines on his face than the typical guy who was still several years from a mid-life crisis.

"Family meeting!" he announced.

His daughter Paige, who was thirteen yet somehow didn't roll her eyes every time her parents spoke, came out of her bedroom. "Did you get pizza?" she asked, pushing up her glasses.

"Yes indeed."

"Is Mom pregnant?"

"What? No!" Boyd glanced at Adeline, who shook her head to verify this.

"So what's the family meeting about?" Adeline asked.

"Let's feast first."

"I'll enjoy it more if I know why you're acting so weird."

"We're going to make a lot of changes," said Boyd. "The first of which is that when I come home in a really good mood with pizza, it shouldn't be seen as 'acting weird.' I want it to be normal."

"Can we have pizza every night from now on?" asked Naomi.

"Nope," said Boyd.

"Are we getting a dog?"

"No. Actually, maybe. We'll discuss that later."

"Is Grandma coming to live with us?"

"God, no."

"I meant the good Grandma."

"I know who you meant. Still, no."

Naomi bunched up her face in concentration as she considered her next question. "Are we going to be on TV?"

"Just let him tell us," said Paige.

"I got a promotion at work," said Boyd. "A really nice one."

"That's great!" said Adeline, giving him a tight hug.

"Oh, honey, I'm so proud of you!"

"The job itself is going to be stressful, but I won't have to take weekend shifts anymore."

"Hooray!" shouted Naomi.

"Will you work in the same building?" asked Adeline.

Boyd shook his head. "Kirkland."

"That's way too far to commute."

"Yep. I know. We're getting out of here. We've been talking about it for a while, and now it's gonna happen. We're getting a house, kids! You'll have your own rooms!"

Paige's face lit up. "Oh my God! Really?"

"Really. I mean, it's not going to be a mansion. It probably won't even be a very big house. But, yes, you'll each have your own room, I promise."

Paige and Naomi joined in the hug. Then everybody dug into the pizza.

"Can I be cyber schooled?" Naomi asked.

"Don't talk with your mouth full," said Adeline.

Naomi swallowed the bite. "Can I?"

"No."

"Mom's still going to work," said Boyd. "She just gets to quit the evil day job that's sucking away her soul. But I'm sure you'll like your new teacher better."

"Ms. Taylor is a b-word."

"I know, sweetie. She's a horrible, horrible woman." Boyd and Adeline made it a point to instill a sense of respect in their daughters...but there was no arguing the fact that Ms. Taylor really was a bitch.

"Can I bring Gordon?"

"Gordon would be happier if you just let him go, don't you think?"

"No!"

"Then yes, you can bring Gordon." Gordon was Naomi's pet tarantula. If Boyd were to rank all of the possible pets he was comfortable having in the house, a tarantula would be dead last. But he hadn't wanted to seem like a coward, so she was allowed to keep Gordon as long as the spider never, ever, ever, ever, ever vacated the aquarium under any circumstances.

"To new beginnings," said Adeline, holding up her can of root beer.

"To new beginnings," they all said, clinking their cans together.

CHAPTER TWO

While Naomi brushed her teeth, or pretended to, Boyd walked into the girls' room and sat down on the edge of Paige's bed.

"You're okay with this, right?" he asked.

Paige pushed up her glasses and nodded. Unlike Naomi, who was a carbon copy of her mother, Paige was almost all recessive traits. She had curly blonde hair that she kept short, in contrast to Adeline and Naomi's shoulder-length straight black hair, and she was the only member of either of their extended families with freckles. No child should have to look like Boyd, so she was fortunate that the resemblance was so faint—just enough that he didn't feel the need for a DNA test. She did have his dimples.

"I know we've discussed it before. I just wanted to make sure your mind hasn't changed."

Paige shrugged.

"Has it?"

"Not really. I mean, I do have some friends now."

"I know," said Boyd. "You'll still get to see them. We'll come back every once in a while."

"We don't need to. They're okay friends. They're not,

like, the best friends ever. I can talk to Chrissy online. I'll be fine."

"And you'll make a lot of new friends, I promise."

"That's not something you can really promise," said Paige, "but yeah, I feel like I will. I'm good. I'm happy to leave."

Boyd was an attentive father, but the mind of a teenage girl was even more of an enigma to him now than it was when he was a teenage boy. He *thought* Paige was okay with the move. Couldn't be sure.

"You know, you'll be able to reinvent yourself," he said. "Get a completely fresh start. Your past can be anything you want. I mean, you shouldn't make stuff up, that's not what I'm saying, but whatever parts you don't like, you don't have to share with anybody."

Paige grinned. "I like that idea."

"This is a rare opportunity. Kids don't get the chance to start from scratch very often."

"Kids move all the time, but I appreciate what you're trying to do for me, Dad."

"I just want to make sure you understand that you do have a say in this."

"So if I threw a screaming fit and started kicking the walls, you wouldn't take the new job?"

"I'd try to reason with you, but if you truly felt that it was worth kicking the walls, I'd tell them to shove their stupid promotion."

"What if I looked at you with puppy dog eyes and said 'Please, dearest Papa, please don't make us move, for I shall be so lonely if we leave'?"

"Oh, with puppy dog eyes you'd definitely get your way."

"What if I threatened to slash my wrists?"

"That's too dark," said Boyd. "Don't say that."

"I'm joking."

"I know you are, sweetie, but let's stick to joking about puppy dog eyes. It stops being fun when you talk about hurting yourself."

"All right. I *was* just kidding, though."

"I know, I know. Your Dad's a wuss. Anyway, I'm going to assume that you're completely on board with the move unless you tell me otherwise."

"I'm completely on board with it. One hundred percent. Because those Kirkland men are *fine*. Mmm mmm mmm. Good luck keeping track of all my boyfriends."

Boyd stood up. "I think that's enough father/daughter time for one evening."

"Are you going to be mad when I come home with a pierced tongue?"

"Goodnight, Paige."

"No, a bisected one."

"Goodnight, Paige."

"If I had a bisected tongue, I could make out with two guys at once. Save some time."

"Why are you so comfortable around me?"

"You should hear what I say around Mom."

"Brush your teeth, Naomi," Boyd called out.

"I am!" said Naomi from the bathroom. "I've been brushing them the whole time! Can't you hear it?"

"You've got your electric toothbrush turned on but you're just holding it in the air. It sounds different when it's against your teeth."

The whirr of the toothbrush changed pitch.

"Thank you."

A moment later the toothbrush stopped and Naomi

walked into the bedroom in her light green nightgown.

"That was five seconds," said Boyd.

Naomi pulled her lips back with her fingers, showing off her teeth. It was actually kind of a creepy sight, but Boyd had to concede that there were no strips of pepperoni hanging from her pearly whites.

"All right, get in bed."

Naomi climbed into bed. Boyd tucked her in and gave her a kiss on the forehead. She didn't ask for stories anymore, and he kind of missed pretending to bicker with her about it.

"Goodnight," he said.

"Goodnight, Daddy," said Naomi.

"Goodnight, Dad," said Paige.

Boyd turned off the light and left the room, shutting the door most but not all the way behind him. He went into the bathroom, brushed his own teeth, and swished some mouthwash. Normally mouthwash was only part of his morning routine, but he was hoping the upbeat mood of the evening would continue after he got into bed.

Adeline was sitting up reading *The Brothers Karamazov* by Dostoevsky. Before that, she'd read a novel where Satan possessed unborn triplets. She made it a point to alternate between trashy reads and highly literary ones. Boyd was also an avid reader, but was happy to stick with lowbrow choices.

He stepped into their bedroom, closed the door, and locked it behind him. Though it had been five years since the moment of horror when Naomi interrupted their lovemaking, the experience had been so upsetting that Boyd now locked the door every time.

"Paige said she wants a bisected tongue so she can make out with two guys at once," Boyd informed her.

"What was the context?"

"Does it matter?"

"I guess not."

"My point is that we have weird children."

"Better than boring children," said Adeline.

"That's true. That's very true." Boyd took off his shirt. There was no need to do it in a seductive manner; Adeline was well acquainted with the just-okay physique that lay beneath. "Anyway, they both seem fine with the move."

"We already knew they would be. You're looking for problems that don't exist."

"I guess. Maybe I'm overcompensating because my parents didn't give a shit what I thought."

"Your dad was military."

"I'm not saying they should've stayed put. I'm just saying that they didn't care if it bothered me."

"The girls get their own bedrooms. We could be moving to the Sahara Desert and they'd be happy. Relax."

"I'm relaxed." Boyd finished undressing and got into bed. He gave Adeline a gentle kiss on the shoulder.

"Yes, we can have sex," said Adeline. "Just let me finish this chapter."

"I can wait."

Boyd assumed that an 1800's Russian novel probably had long chapters, so he picked up the crime thriller he'd been reading. But he was so excited about the new job and home that he couldn't focus on any of the words. Honestly, his level of excitement made him feel a little guilty that he hadn't taken a more proactive approach to getting out of here sooner.

Oh well. Didn't matter now.

A few minutes later, Adeline set her book aside, and they had passionate but quiet sex.

- - -

They didn't have much credit card debt, but what miniscule savings they had was meant for the girls' college education. Right now it wasn't even enough for textbooks. So putting a down payment on a home would be virtually impossible. In a year, with a healthier bank account, they'd revisit the issue. For now, they decided to rent.

Boyd and Adeline did the online portion of the house hunting together, but he did the in-person part by himself, since it was a four-hour drive to Kirkland and he had to spend a week there for his class. They weren't *that* fussy, but the new place did have to be near good schools and away from crack houses.

The market for a three-bedroom rental home in Kirkland was not as great as he would have hoped. There were numerous deal breakers as he searched. Often he only needed to drive past a home to remove it from the list. For example, though it was entirely possible that the gentleman urinating on the front porch would never urinate on that particular front porch again, it was impossible to shake the first impression. Another home had standing water in the front yard even though it hadn't rained in the three days Boyd had been in town.

Other homes were ruled out after an inside tour. Though Boyd wouldn't be opposed to eventually buying a fixer-upper, he didn't want to rent one, and the landlord's promise that the owner would "get around to fixing those electrical sockets soon" was not reassuring.

A gradual lowering of his standards throughout the week didn't help.

Still other homes looked perfect, but were off the market by the time Boyd was able to talk to somebody on the phone.

By Thursday evening, he was starting to get discouraged, though he didn't confess this to Adeline. At least the training was going well. The class focused more on a corporate environment than what Boyd would be working in, but he was picking up some helpful tips and was confident in his ability to effectively boss people around.

Class ended early on Friday. He received a certificate suitable for framing. If the search for a place to live went on past today, he'd be responsible for his own hotel costs, and he was anxious to get back to Adeline and the girls, so hopefully this would be the day.

When he looked at the first place on that day's list, he had a good feeling.

CHAPTER THREE

*I*t definitely wasn't perfect. Much of the light blue paint on the outside was peeling, and there were anthills all over the yard. But *what* a yard. Boyd would've been okay with a home where you could open your window and hand your neighbor a cup of coffee through their window, but this place had a fenced-in yard the size of the swimming pool at the YMCA. He could imagine having dozens of friends over for a barbecue. Naomi would absolutely *love* it, and Paige would be impressed as well.

The houses on each side were close enough that it would be a problem if the neighbors liked to blast loud music late at night, and it wasn't as if Boyd could walk around his backyard naked—not that he would—but this home had an amazing amount of privacy.

And there was a koi pond. A frickin' koi pond! There were no fish in it at the moment, but Boyd could never have imagined that a home with a koi pond in the backyard would be within their price range. The upper end of their price range, yet still...

He was getting too excited. He hadn't even seen the inside of the house yet. There might be snakes slithering through holes in the walls.

He wandered around the outside of the house, looking for defects, until he heard a car pull into the driveway. Three o'clock. The landlord was exactly on time for their walkthrough. Boyd hurried to the front yard to greet him.

The landlord was a short man with a thin mustache and hair that stuck up in the back. He was dressed in slacks and a white dress shirt with heavy sweat stains on the sides. He wiped his right hand off on his pants before extending it to Boyd.

"Mr. Gardner?"

"Yep." Boyd shook his hand.

"Jack Ponter. Sorry I'm late."

"You're not late."

Jack took his cell phone out of his pocket, glanced at the display, then shoved it back into his pocket again. "Oh, good. Did you get a chance to look around outside?"

Boyd nodded. "Koi pond. I love it."

Jack grinned. "Oh, yeah. I don't have one at my current home, but I did in the home before that, and it's very relaxing. Almost hypnotic. I could sit out there for hours and just watch the fish. But don't make the mistake that the previous renters here did. They're real fish. You do have to feed them."

"They didn't feed the fish?"

"No. It was a real shame. What a waste."

"I assure you that if we end up living here, we'll take care of the fish." Actually, Boyd had no idea how much koi fish cost. Were they ridiculously expensive? He couldn't imagine that a few really big goldfish were out of his price range, but he'd never researched the subject.

Jack reached into his other pocket and took out a key

ring. He found the correct one after a couple of tries and unlocked the front door. "After you," he said, pushing it open.

Boyd walked into the house. Unlike the outside, the inside looked newly painted. Not the most aesthetically pleasing shade of yellow, but they could certainly live with it for a year. Hardwood floors—Adeline would love that.

"Mind if I take pictures for my wife?" asked Boyd.

"Oh, no, go right ahead. Take as many as you want. Is it just you two or do you have kids?"

"Two daughters."

"How old?"

"Eight and thirteen."

Jack chuckled. "I've got a fifteen-year-old. You've got some interesting times ahead, my friend."

"Already there."

"Well, as you probably saw in the listing, this place has three bedrooms and two baths, so there's plenty of space." Jack gestured around the large room they were in. "This is the living room. Cable-ready. Lots of light." He began to pull the cords to raise the blinds, letting in sunlight that revealed all of the dust in the air.

"Beautiful," said Boyd. He was imaginative in many ways, but it was difficult for him to envision what this empty room would look like fully furnished. That was Adeline's job. He took a few pictures from different angles.

"It's got a nice open floor plan," said Jack, leading Boyd through the rest of the house. "No narrow hallways to make you feel claustrophobic. You and your wife can have the master bedroom, which has a bathroom attached, and then there are two smaller bedrooms."

Each of the "smaller" bedrooms was bigger than the room that Paige and Naomi currently shared. The girls were going to be in paradise.

Boyd walked into what might be Paige's bedroom and opened the closet door.

"None of the closets are very big," Jack admitted. "I guess this house was built at a time when people had less stuff."

"When was it built?"

"1920's, I think. It's still got the original refrigerator. No, I'm kidding. Let's check out the kitchen."

The kitchen was spacious. Luxurious, even. At least three times as much counter space as their apartment, and cabinets galore. Dishwasher, microwave, and one of those stovetops where the burners were underneath the surface. Very nice. Boyd took more pictures.

"Plenty of room to spread out when you're making a meal," said Jack. "Who does the cooking in your family?"

"My wife does the *good* cooking. I'm the macaroni and cheese guy. We eat a lot of macaroni and cheese."

"Well, if you want to elevate your mac and cheese like they do in those cooking competition shows, you've got all kinds of room for it. Do you watch those?"

"Nah."

"They're weirdly addicting. It's amazing how much suspense they can wring out of a judge cutting into a steak to see if it's medium rare. Is it overdone? Is it underdone? And then they always go to a commercial break. Anyway, it's a roomy kitchen."

"It sure is," said Boyd.

"And here's the second bathroom, which is also your laundry room. The washer and dryer are kind of old, so you can keep them here or bring in your own."

"We'll keep them," said Boyd. Adeline had never minded using the apartment complex's laundry room, because it gave her time to read while waiting for the machines to finish, but this would be so much more convenient.

"Any questions so far?"

"How are the schools in this area?"

"Excellent. I can only personally speak to my daughter's high school, but all of the schools around here have high ratings. It's a great area for kids to grow up. And you're not going to have any issues with the neighbors. Everybody pretty much keeps to themselves." Jack wiped some sweat off his forehead. "I suppose you could see that as a negative. If you're hoping for block parties or neighbors stopping by with freshly baked apple pies, you'll be disappointed."

"As long as my daughters make friends, I'm happy."

"I'm sure they will. I'd bring Sarah over, but at that age, two years apart might as well be twenty."

"They'll be fine. Hell, Naomi can make friends in the checkout line at the grocery store."

Jack wiped his forehead again. "Obviously, the place does have working A/C. It just doesn't make sense to keep it on while nobody's living here."

"I totally understand. Can I see the attic? That's where I loved to play when we visited my grandmother."

"That's not going to happen in this one, I'm afraid. I'm more than happy to show it to you, but you can't really walk around up there or store much of anything. You'll go up there to change the air filter and that's about it."

"No need to show me. I believe you."

"Now I feel like I should show you just so you don't

think it's full of bats or bat guano or something." They walked back to the living room. In the alcove between the living room and bathroom, there was a trapdoor in the ceiling. Jack reached up and pulled on the cord. After the trapdoor swung down, he unfolded the aluminum ladder.

Boyd looked up into the darkness. No bats flew out. "I trust you on the guano."

Jack folded the ladder and the trapdoor swung up to the closed position. "The basement is a different story. I don't mean that it has bats; I mean that you can actually spend time down there."

They returned to the kitchen. Jack opened the door to the basement and flipped on a light switch. Boyd followed him down the wooden stairs. The basement had a pleasant...well, *basement* smell. Musty. Probably not a smell that most people enjoyed. Unlike the main floor of the house, the basement was furnished. There were a couple of empty bookshelves, a couch that had not been fashionable for a very long time, an empty television stand, a recliner, and a ping-pong table.

"This is where you'll find your hot water heater, and it's got a nice-sized pantry." Jack swung open a wooden door to reveal an empty pantry that would indeed hold more food than Boyd could ever imagine having in the house. Maybe they could start buying in bulk. "The previous tenants abandoned the furniture down here because I think they just didn't want to deal with trying to get it up the stairs. We'd have it removed if you wanted it gone. It's kind of fun to have a ping-pong table down here, though they took the paddles and balls."

"Adeline wouldn't like that couch, but she wouldn't be down here much anyway."

"It's a good place for teenagers to get into trouble."

"That's not really a selling point."

"Let me rephrase. It's a good place for teenagers to get into trouble, but not *too* much trouble, because they know you could come down those stairs at any time. If they're smoking pot, you'll know it."

Boyd took a few pictures.

"Or," said Jack, "you can set yourself up a decent man-cave."

"Pretty sure I wouldn't be able to claim the whole basement. Hey, do you have another appointment? Do you have to go?"

Jack shook his head. "This basement is nice and cool. I'm in no hurry to leave."

"If you're not in a rush, I'd like to send these pictures to my wife and make sure she doesn't want me to ask you anything."

"Go right ahead."

Boyd was pleased to see that he got a signal down here. He tapped away at his screen. "Any secret history to this place I should know about?"

"No axe murders, if that's what you're asking. At least, none that I'm aware of."

"Happy to hear it. I'd noticed that it hadn't been rented for a few months."

"Oh, that. The people who lived here before...they weren't great tenants. I don't mean that they ripped up the floorboards or anything. They just didn't take care of the place. Took the owner a long time and a lot of cash to get the house back into shape. It's still far from perfect—I mean, I would've painted the outside."

"That's no big deal."

"So that was a bad experience for her, and she quite

frankly priced it out of the market for a while. People came and looked, but koi pond or not, she simply wasn't going to rent it out for that price. It didn't seem to bother her. Recently, I guess she—it's not my place to talk about her personal business, but she had a bit of a financial stumbling block and needed somebody paying rent here right away. I think she went a little too far in the other direction."

"I'm surprised nobody else is looking at it," said Boyd.

"I'm sorry, did I give that impression? No, no, I've given a few tours today. There's at least one application in. The owner doesn't want cats scratching the place up, and they've got two of 'em, so I think if you passed the credit check your family would get it over theirs, but I wouldn't wait too long."

"Oh. Okay, well, I've sent the pictures, so let me call—"

His phone rang.

"It's my wife. Mind if I take this?"

"Of course not."

"Hi, honey," Boyd said.

"That's an amazing backyard," said Adeline.

"Yeah. The whole house is definitely workable. It meets all of our criteria, plus it's got the basement and the ping-pong table. I say we go for it."

"The girls loved the pictures. They're already fighting about which room they get."

"Tell them the decision is out of their control. If you're okay with it, I'll get the process started here." Boyd wanted to ask her to do some research on the schools, with the understanding that they'd withdraw their application if Adeline wasn't satisfied, but he didn't want to say that out loud with Jack standing right there.

He'd text it to her.

"I'm okay with it," said Adeline, "but I want to check out the schools online before we officially commit."

"Sounds great. Give the girls a kiss for me."

Boyd disconnected the call. "We're in," he told Jack. "What's the next step?"

- - -

They got the house.

CHAPTER FOUR
BEFORE

"You got a problem with my colostomy bag?"

The kid didn't look away from it. "Nah. Just don't see a lot of them. That thing permanent?"

Larry Maddox shook his head. "Recovering from surgery."

"Oh yeah? What kind?"

"The kind where you crap in a plastic sack afterward."

The kid grinned and took a long drink of his beer, finishing off the pint. Maddox hated that he was old enough to think of a twenty-two year-old as a "kid," but there wasn't shit he could do to stop the passage of time. And, hey, he'd never expected to live past thirty, much less forty, so even if he felt old as hell at least he wasn't dead and buried.

The kid wiped his mouth off on the back of his sleeve and belched. "This is an intense job. You can still work, right?"

"I wouldn't be here if I couldn't, Eddie."

"Edwin."

"Really?"

"That surprise you?"

"Yeah. I thought I'd get shot if I called you Edwin.

Most guys like you would be Eddie all the way."

"Well, I ain't like most guys like me."

Maddox did not actually believe he'd get shot if he called the kid Edwin. Oh, the kid might *try* something, but being twenty years Maddox's junior wouldn't save him if they each decided that the other needed to die.

"So what have you got for me, Edwin?"

Edwin glanced around the bar to make sure nobody was listening in on their conversation, then he picked up a briefcase and set it on the table. That redneck dipshit didn't look like he'd carried a briefcase in his life.

He unlocked the case, opened the lid, and handed Maddox a picture. He could've just had it in an envelope. Must've thought he was in a spy thriller or something.

Maddox picked up the picture. It was of a blonde woman, probably in her early fifties. The bad facelift added more years than it subtracted.

"Sure, we can kill her, no problem."

"Rad."

"Is the word 'rad' back in use?"

"It is with me."

"Your boss doesn't have his own guys who could do this?"

Edwin shook his head. "If his guys did it, it'd look like something his guys did. He can't have that for this job."

"That's reasonable. Any challenges I should know about?"

"Nah. She lives alone. No security system. Just a dog."

"I'm not going to kill the dog."

"Nobody's asking you to kill the dog."

"I mean it," said Maddox. "Under no circumstances will I harm a dog. I'll let an orphanage full of babies burn to death before I do anything bad to a dog."

"It's one of those shitty little yappy dogs."

"Don't care."

"You guys aren't going to have to hurt it. She keeps it tied up in the backyard most of the time. Of course, if you kill its owner, the poor thing's gonna starve to death."

"I'll worry about that part. Anyway, yeah, we're happy to finish off this hag," said Maddox. "Seems straightforward enough."

"There's a little more to it," said Edwin. "It needs to be horrific. I mean, truly ghastly. We don't want it to look like a hit job. We want it to look like a thrill kill. When people see the mess they need to go '*Holy Jesus fuck!*'"

"Gotcha."

"'*What kind of sickos would do such a thing? Oh, God, what has this world come to?*' We want them to question the very idea that there is goodness in the world. We want them to think you popped a boner when you did it."

"We can handle that," said Maddox. "Not our usual style, but we're flexible." He'd wondered why they wanted three of them to kill one old lady. Now it made a little more sense.

"And can you make it funny?"

"Funny?"

"A gory sight gag. A sick joke. You know, a visual pun or something. I can't think of an example off the top of my head."

"Think harder."

"You could write something witty in her blood. Or, like, cut off her head and shove a stuffed hamster in her mouth."

"Would that be funny?"

"Not ha-ha funny, but it would be worth a chuckle, I think. I'm just spitballing."

"Are you providing the hamster?"

"It doesn't have to be a hamster. I'm not supposed to be the idea guy here. That's why we're paying you."

"Amusing massacre," said Maddox. "Got it. You understand that if my partners and I go absolutely batshit on this lady, it's going to be national news, right? It increases our risk if we can't do it quickly and quietly, and that increases your cost."

Edwin shook his head. "You don't have to worry about that. It'll be cleaned up before any cops are on the scene. As long as you don't tweet about it, you're safe."

Maddox shrugged. "All right. You'll get your hilarious slaughter. Did you bring the first half of our payment?"

"Of course." Edwin glanced around the bar again. Maddox half-expected him to pick up another briefcase, but instead he took out a thick letter-sized envelope and slid it across the table. Maddox quickly slid it onto his lap. No need to count the money. If they were going to try to rip him off, they'd do it with the final payment. "All the other information you'll need is in there, too."

"Consider it done."

"You're sure that...bag isn't going to be a problem?" asked Edwin.

"My partners do most of the work. I'm the brains of the trio."

It wasn't a real colostomy bag. It was filled with water and chewing tobacco, which concealed a knife. Maddox had come up with the idea a few months ago before a meeting with a lowlife. He knew he'd be searched and wanted to make sure he didn't find himself defenseless if the scumbag's goons tried to take him out. He'd been secretly disappointed when the meeting ended without an attempt on his life.

He continued to use the trick at future meetings, even when nobody was going to search him. Hell, he had a perfectly good revolver tucked into his inside jacket pocket right now. But one day he'd tear open that bag and jam the knife into somebody's throat, and their shocked expression before the blade sunk into their neck would be worth the wait.

- - -

Three days later, around one in the morning, he sat in a car with Heck (who you could call Hector if you wanted to lose an eye) and Fletcher. They'd been parked in front of the house for about ten minutes.

"What do you think?" Maddox asked.

"Seems okay," said Heck.

Fletcher said nothing. He wasn't much of a talker, which is why he always sat in the back. He *could* talk, quite eloquently, but the big creepy bald fucker looked like he might only communicate through grunts. He was a valuable asset to the team when they needed to intimidate somebody. Usually they didn't—most of their jobs were simple B&E. A murder like tonight was a rare treat.

Heck was also creepy looking, though in a more subtle way, like a neighbor you'd wave to in the morning but wouldn't let babysit your children. He was ridiculously skinny and his fingers were double-jointed. The guy was constantly bending them backwards, and Maddox was constantly telling him to knock that shit off.

"Let's give it five more minutes," said Maddox.

Something didn't feel quite right. It was nothing he could pinpoint; there was certainly no evidence that anybody was awake inside the house. Nothing specific that should've made him nervous. Waiting another five minutes probably wouldn't offer new insight, and in fact it would increase the chances of the lady getting up to take a piss or something. But something was off. He'd decide if he still felt that way a few minutes from now.

"Why?" asked Heck.

"Just because."

"All right." Heck grinned, exposing teeth that were too straight and white to go with his pallid complexion. He looked like the kind of guy whose teeth should be rotting out of his head. "Decide what you're going to do to her yet?"

"Nah." They'd brought knives, and a gun in case things got out of hand, but for the most part they'd agreed to make creative use of whatever was available inside the house. "Trying not to think about it. I don't want to mess with the spontaneity."

"I've got some bad, bad, bad ideas," said Heck. "I may need you and Fletcher to wait in another room for a while. Give me some privacy."

"No rape," said Maddox.

"What do you mean, no rape?"

"What are you, a frat boy? What do you think I mean by that?"

"Is that their rule?"

"It's my rule."

"Jesus. No harm to animals, no sexual assault, no kids..."

"I never said no kids," Maddox corrected.

"Yeah, you did."

"Nope. There's never been a 'no kid' rule."

"You'd kill a little kid?" Heck asked.

"I wouldn't go out of my way to kill a kid, but I don't have a personal rule against it."

"That's fucked up."

"I like animals more than I like crappy little kids. What's so shocking about that? Are you saying you wouldn't harm a child?"

"Oh, I'd kill a kid, no problem," said Heck. "But I'd also kill a cat and bang a chick who didn't want it. You've got a weird-ass moral code."

"I'd kill a kid," said Fletcher from the back.

"Good," said Maddox. "We're all in agreement on that issue. But since there's not a kid inside that house, it doesn't matter. Nobody gets alone time with her tonight. It's too risky."

"How is it risky?" asked Heck.

"It's risky because you'd be distracted. You can't tell me that you could be inside her and still fully aware of your environment."

Heck shrugged. "What's she gonna do about it?"

"She could grab a goddamn vase off the floor and bash you over the head while you were pounding her."

"Not if I did it after we got rid of her arms. Legs, too. I don't mind if she's a torso."

"Are you messing with me right now?" asked Maddox.

"I'm just saying."

"Without arms and legs she could still take a bite out of your face."

Heck nodded. "That's hot."

"All right, all right, so you're basically admitting that you're just screwing around. Nice. Real nice. Heck the stand-up comedian. That's what we need before a dangerous job."

"Three of us against one lady? How is that dangerous? This would be easy even if it was a solo job."

Fletcher leaned forward. "Are we going in, or are we going to yap all night?"

Something still felt wrong to Maddox, but he couldn't yet explain to himself why he felt this way, much less articulate it to his partners. It was important to trust your gut. But it was also important not to squander a big (and desperately needed) payday over an uneasy feeling that you couldn't justify. He could probably get away with postponing it a night, but what good would that do? He might feel the same way tomorrow.

"Maddox?" asked Heck.

"This feels wrong."

"How?"

"Just wrong."

"Like, *morally* wrong...?"

"Nah. Never mind. It's nothing. Let's go in there and make a mess."

CHAPTER FIVE

Adeline had read that moving was one of the top five stressors in a person's life. So, yes, the fact that she loved every minute of it was very strange.

She *enjoyed* packing up her possessions. Enjoyed going through kitchen drawers and discovering utensils she hadn't seen in five years. Enjoyed the game of trying to maximize every inch of space in each cardboard box. Hell, she enjoyed the sound of taping a box closed.

Though they were moving to a larger place and could bring all of their clutter with them if they wanted, Adeline enjoyed the process of getting rid of stuff they no longer (or never had) needed. Considering the size of their apartment, it was amazing how much was in the Goodwill donation pile.

Okay, she supposed that she didn't enjoy trying to keep Paige and Naomi focused on the task at hand. Naomi in particular didn't want to get rid of anything, even possessions that had been under her bed since before she started grade school. But despite the occasional daughter difficulties, Adeline found herself humming, whistling, or even singing through the entire process.

Her favorite part, of course, was getting to quit her office job. She'd given them the proper two weeks' notice, her resignation letter contained no profanity, and on her final day she'd casually walked out of the building instead of setting it on fire, but it was still a supremely satisfying experience. Yes, pretty much as soon as they got settled in Kirkland she'd have to start looking for a new job, which wouldn't be fun, but she'd worry about that when the time came. For now, she was just the bizarre mom who loved packing.

On a Friday morning, as they walked through the empty apartment one last time, she did get a bit choked up. They went from room to room, each family member sharing their favorite memories from each one. She was pretty sure Boyd fibbed about his favorite bedroom memory; she certainly did. Naomi cried as they left.

Boyd drove the U-Haul truck and Naomi rode with him, while Adeline and Paige followed. It would've been nice if Paige was three years older, because she could have driven their second car instead of Boyd towing it with the U-Haul, which made Adeline nervous even when she wasn't driving directly behind it.

While Boyd dealt with a presumed barrage of questions from Naomi, Adeline and Paige listened to music. Paige had promised to take her mother's musical tastes into consideration when compiling the playlist, but Adeline didn't think she'd done a very good job.

Four and a half hours later (thanks to several more bathroom stops than they'd scheduled) they arrived at their new home. It looked neither better nor worse than the pictures. Though it was definitely not their forever home, it seemed to be a perfectly good place to start their new life.

When Adeline asked how Naomi had done on the drive over, Boyd just gave her a pained smile.

They'd briefly toyed with the idea of hiring professional movers for an hour or so, just to help unload the U-Haul, then decided it was an unnecessary cost. Now that they were unloading on a ridiculously hot day, even for summer, Adeline wished they hadn't spared that particular expense. It wasn't as if an eight-year-old could help carry in her own bed.

Eventually all of the furniture and every carefully labeled box was in the proper room. They all sat in the living room, resting.

"When can we get our fish?" Naomi asked.

"Not for a while," Boyd told her. "Maybe next week. We've got a lot of other stuff to take care of first."

"Can I decorate my room any way I want?"

"As long as you keep your room clean, yes," said Adeline. "You're off to a fresh start. You've got a totally spotless room. If you try to keep it that way, tidying it up will never be a big deal, and you won't get grounded. Think of how amazing it would be to have your room a couple minutes away from being clean at all times. You'd never have to miss TV shows because you were being punished. This could be a whole new experience for you."

"Ha ha," said Naomi.

"I'm not kidding. This is your chance to always have a clean room."

"I don't like it when my room is clean."

"Then I guess the yelling and grounding will continue."

"I'm going to have pictures of naked men all over my wall," said Paige.

"That's fine," said Adeline. "As long as you keep them tidy."

"I don't mean pictures where they're in shadows and stuff. You'll be able to see everything."

"That's not a problem. You're thirteen. I can't make you decorate your room with tasteful pictures."

"Tasty pictures, maybe."

"I guess I'll have a reason to come into your room more often."

"Can I have naked pictures on my wall?" asked Naomi.

"Not until you're nine."

"They're going to be in ball gags," said Paige.

"Enough!" said Boyd, who was adorable when he was embarrassed. "Knock it off, all of you. Paige, no more Internet for you."

"I didn't learn about ball gags from the Internet."

"Then where did you—don't tell me."

"I learned it from—"

"I said don't tell me."

"What's a ball gag?" asked Naomi.

"Remember that scene in *Pulp Fiction?*"

"When the hell did you two watch *Pulp Fiction?*" asked Boyd.

"Paige, stop messing with your father," said Adeline. "The girls outnumber the boys in this house and it's not fair to make him uncomfortable."

"I'm not uncomfortable," said Boyd.

"You're sweating."

"We've been carrying boxes all day. No dad should have to listen to his daughter talk about gags."

"Ball gags," Paige corrected.

"Stop it."

"I'm sure you and Mom have one packed up in one of these boxes somewhere."

"Dad said to stop it," Adeline told her. "You always have to take these things one step too far, don't you?"

"Only one step?" asked Boyd.

Adeline ignored him and continued to talk to Paige. "When you're talking, imagine a big red line in the air, and each time you think of a funny comment try to decide if it's above the line or under the line. If it's above the line, think of a different comment."

"Don't you want me to be edgy?"

"You can be edgy around your friends."

Ouch. What a terrible comment immediately after moving her daughter away from her hard-to-acquire friends. *Great job, Mom. Nice going.*

"Sorry," said Adeline. "I meant—"

Paige pushed up her glasses. "I know. It's fine."

Adeline started to apologize further, then decided to let this drop instead of digging herself further into a hole. It was challenging for Paige to make friends but not impossible. And that might all change in this new environment.

"Dad said I could reinvent myself here," said Paige.

"He's right."

"So can I get rid of these ugly glasses?"

"You mean laser eye surgery?"

Paige shook her head. "Just contacts."

The glasses weren't ugly at all; they were actually quite flattering on her, and Paige had loved them when they picked them out last year. Adeline knew that new frames weren't the answer. "Sure, if that's what you want. Can you handle touching your eyeball?"

Paige grinned and extended her index finger.

"We'll take you to the optometrist and see what they say. We can probably switch you over to contacts before school starts."

Normally this was something she and Boyd would discuss before making a promise to their daughter, but he was right there in the room and not shy about exercising his veto power. There was no reason, in this case, for a "We'll talk about it later" response.

"Thanks, Mom."

"Can I get contacts too?" asked Naomi.

"Your eyes are fine," said Boyd. "Be thankful."

"Can I have Paige's old glasses?"

"They'll give you a headache," Paige told her.

"Not if I take the lenses out."

"We don't need to figure this out right now," said Adeline. "We'll make sure everybody's happy with their eyeballs."

"I think we should celebrate our first night in our new house," said Boyd. "Who's hungry?"

Paige, Naomi, and Adeline raised their hands.

"How about burgers?"

"McDonald's?" Naomi asked.

"Nope," said Boyd. "We're going to find the biggest, greasiest, cheesiest, most bacon-covered burgers in town."

At some point, Adeline knew that she'd have to put a stop to celebrations that involved junk food, but tonight, big greasy cheesy bacon-covered burgers sounded fantastic.

- - -

Their fries were covered with melted cheese and bacon

bits, and this place had four different flavors of ketchup. The Gardner family was going to do well here.

- - -

Boyd and Adeline each gave Naomi a kiss on the cheek as they tucked her into bed. "Do you want us to leave the door open?" Adeline asked.

"No, that's okay," said Naomi.

"Really?"

"I've got Gordon to protect me."

The tarantula's aquarium rested on the dresser next to Naomi's bed. Paige had insisted that the aquarium be on the other side of the room, but now that Naomi had her own bedroom, she could keep it wherever she wanted.

"And I'm sure he'll do a great job," said Adeline. "Let us know if you need anything."

"I will."

Adeline and Boyd left the room, shutting the door behind them.

"Fuckin' spider," said Boyd in a whisper.

"He's a perfectly good pet."

"What's wrong with a gerbil? Or a lizard? Or even a hermit crab? Hermit crabs are miniature monsters; why not have one of those?"

"She likes her tarantula."

"I know she likes it, but why? I mean, even with something like a boa constrictor you could say that you enjoyed having it slither around your neck. A spider doesn't do anything for you except crawl around being scary."

"Maybe she'll outgrow it."

"Or maybe this is just the beginning. We'll have

grandchildren who sleep in web cocoons."

"I'm going to take a wild guess and say that we probably won't."

"It better not get out," said Boyd.

"It never has."

"I will stomp that spider under my shoe if I ever see it running loose. You can explain to our daughter that Daddy murdered her pet."

"You're not wearing shoes right now," said Adeline. "Would you stomp it with your bare feet?"

"Don't even joke about that."

"It might goosh up between your toes."

"Funny."

"What kind of sound would Gordon make? Do you think it's a soft squish or something more crunchy?"

"This is why we have a daughter who talks about ball gags."

"You knew the genetics when you married me."

Boyd kissed her on the lips. "I assumed that my phobias would be off-limits."

"I know where the red line in the air is."

There was a cough from Naomi's bedroom.

"She's well aware that you're going to pluck Gordon's legs off if he gets out of the aquarium," said Adeline. "He won't get out."

"I'm not going to rip its legs off. I wouldn't torture it. I'd kill it quickly."

Naomi coughed again.

"You okay, sweetie?" Adeline called out.

"Yes," Naomi said. Then she coughed some more.

Adeline and Boyd walked back to her bedroom and opened the door. "What's wrong?"

"Nothing."

"Is it the dust?"

"Maybe." Naomi put her hand over her mouth and coughed.

"Cough into your arm," said Adeline, reflexively, even though Naomi wouldn't be shaking hands with anybody to spread germs.

Naomi coughed into her arm, more violently than before.

"Do you want a glass of water?" Boyd asked.

Naomi nodded. Boyd left the room. Then Naomi began coughing with such intensity—entire body shaking, tears pouring down her cheeks—that Adeline suddenly became genuinely worried.

It was okay. Just a cough. Coughing meant she was breathing, so it wasn't as if she was choking or anything like that. There wasn't really anything she could do (you weren't actually supposed to pat somebody on the back when they were coughing) except put a reassuring hand on her knee.

When Boyd returned, Naomi's coughing had subsided. She took the glass from him and drank most of the water in one swig. She belched and then took a couple of deep breaths.

"I'm sorry," she said.

"You don't have to be sorry. Are you okay?"

"Yeah. I just coughed."

"We need to get rid of the dust tomorrow," Adeline told Boyd.

"They were supposed to vacuum out the air ducts before we got here. Maybe they didn't. We'll get it all taken care of."

"I'm okay now," said Naomi.

"I'm glad." Adeline kissed her on the forehead. "You

gave us a little scare."

They walked out of the room again. This time Adeline left the door open a crack.

CHAPTER SIX

Via text message, Jack claimed that they had indeed vacuumed the air ducts before their arrival. After about twenty minutes trying to figure out where the hell they'd packed the flashlight, Boyd peered into the duct and had to admit that there were no dust bunnies to be seen. Nor could he see dust in the air when he opened the shades in the living room.

Naomi having a brief coughing fit didn't mean that the house was filled with particles, but still, they'd be sure to give the place a thorough dusting as part of today's work.

The whole family was in a good mood as they unpacked and turned this house into a home. By the end of the day, as Boyd flopped onto the couch, he couldn't believe how much they'd accomplished. There was a lot left to do, but if they carried the unpacked boxes down into the basement, and didn't go into the kitchen or bathrooms, and ignored the bare walls, there was almost the illusion that they hadn't just moved in yesterday.

By the end of the next day, it was really starting to feel like their home. Maybe it wouldn't if Adeline, Paige and Naomi weren't right there with him; Boyd still couldn't find anything, and he kept noticing little imperfections like nicks on the doors and paint specks on the floorboards. But they *were* there, and so it did.

Now Boyd just had to hope that he liked his job.

On Monday morning, he got up, took a long hot shower, and put on his slacks, dress shirt, and tie. This was not a slacks, dress shirt, or tie kind of job, but since it was his first day, he wanted to make a good impression on his employees.

"I didn't know you knew how to tie a tie," said Adeline, putting her arms around him as he looked in the mirror.

"Yep." Boyd did not know how to tie a tie. This was a zipper tie, which required no knowledge of Windsor knots or whatever the hell they were called.

"You're going to do great."

"I'm supposed to kick somebody's ass on the first day, right?"

"You're thinking of prison."

"Oh, yeah."

"You'll do fine," Adeline assured him again.

"You're acting like I'm really nervous about it."

"Aren't you?"

Boyd shook his head. "It's just a job."

"All jobs are nerve-wracking on your first day. Don't get me wrong; I'm not trying to make you nervous. If you're not nervous, that's great. You're good with people and you know your stuff. I'll stop talking now."

The girls' school didn't start for a couple of weeks, so they'd spend the day working on the house with Adeline, but after today they'd be more or less released from their unpacking duties to enjoy what remained of the summer.

"Whoa, Dad!" said Paige as Boyd and Adeline walked into the dining room. "I didn't know your new job was being a fashion model."

"Thank you."

"Do you have to wear that every day?"

"Nope. Just making a good impression."

"You sure will."

Boyd couldn't decide if Paige was being genuine or sarcastic. He decided that she was being genuine and gave her a hug.

Adeline took four bowls down from the cabinet and set them on the counter. Then she took out a box of cereal and some packets of oatmeal. "The breakfast buffet is ready," she announced.

Boyd added raisins to his oatmeal because he was in a fancy mood, and the four of them sat down to eat. Naomi took an oversized bite of her cold cereal and scowled.

"What's wrong?" Boyd asked.

"It tastes gross."

He leaned over and sniffed the bowl. "Oh, yeah, the milk has gone bad."

"I just bought it," said Adeline. She leaned over to sniff it as well, apparently in case Boyd and Naomi didn't know what sour milk smelled like. She got up and took the gallon jug out of the refrigerator. "This isn't even close to expired yet."

"You think the refrigerator's broken?" Boyd asked.

Adeline reached inside and felt some items from their meager selection. "Everything else is cold."

"It could've gone out long enough to kill the milk and then turned on again."

"Maybe." She picked up Naomi's bowl and poured the contents into the sink.

"At least it wasn't chunky," said Paige.

"Do you want some oatmeal?" Adeline asked Naomi.

"Ew, no."

"We don't have many choices, kiddo. I haven't done a big shopping trip yet."

"Can I have toast?"

"We don't have any jelly, just butter."

"That's okay."

Adeline rinsed the cereal bowl out thoroughly, then opened one of the cabinets and took out a loaf of bread. She removed a couple of pieces from the bag. "Aw, goddamn it."

"What?" asked Boyd.

Adeline held the pieces of bread up to him. There was a distinct streak of mold running along the sides.

"Lovely."

"The package says it's fresh through the 17th."

Boyd shrugged. "So we went to a crappy grocery store. Better than finding out our refrigerator's broken."

"I wonder if we should throw out everything we bought from them? If both the milk and the bread are bad, anything else could be, too."

"That's probably a good idea. We'll get rid of everything that wasn't pre-packaged. I don't know about you, but I don't know what spoiled orange juice tastes like, so we should play it safe."

"I'm going to get a refund," said Adeline.

"Don't worry about it. We only bought enough to keep us going for a couple of days."

"But they should know that they're selling rotten food."

"However you want to handle it is fine with me," said Boyd. "I'm just saying that we're okay if we need to re-buy a few groceries."

"You should make them drink the milk," said Paige.

"Yeah," said Naomi.

"It seemed like a perfectly good store," said Adeline. "This is pretty disappointing."

"We're not living in the pioneer days where we have to ride two days in a horse-drawn carriage to get our rations for the winter," said Boyd. "It's not a big deal if the first grocery store we tried sucks."

"Yeah, yeah, I know," said Adeline. "It's just frustrating."

"Then maybe Paige is right. March back into the store, find the manager, and bash him over the head with the jug. Then jam a funnel into his mouth and pour every last blob of that milk in. Make sure the city of Kirkland knows that *nobody* sells Adeline Gardner bad milk."

"I'd just planned to have them take a whiff, but your idea does have appeal."

"No, what you should do is make a really delicious looking peanut butter and jelly sandwich, and bring it in and pretend that you're offering a gift because you had such a positive shopping experience. And then when the manager is chewing and realizes that something's not right, you scream 'I bought this bread from you! How do you like it, huh? How do you like it?' It'll be fun. Thanks to my new job, we can afford to post bail."

"Dad's weird," said Naomi.

"*You're* weird."

"I know."

"Anyway, I have to get going," said Boyd, pushing back his chair. "I hope all three of you have a nice productive day, and that when I come back this place looks like a royal palace."

"We'll get right on that," said Adeline.

"Don't work too hard."

"You, either. No, wait..."

- - -

It was a pretty good first day as a supervisor. The new job was eight miles from home instead of the five that he was used to, but he didn't spend the whole commute stuck in traffic, so the drive was far less maddening.

He was responsible for about a dozen employees, a number that would gradually increase over the next few months if everything went well. Boyd thought he'd made a solid connection with them, trying to give off sort of an "I'm here to be your boss and not your friend, but that doesn't mean we can't also be friends" vibe. He'd quickly identified a couple of slackers he'd have to watch more closely than the others, and also his achievement-seeking superstars. He could definitely work with this group of people.

He even had his own office. Not a big office. Not a luxurious office. Not even an office with a door. Still, it made him feel like a bigwig. Boyd Gardner, VIP.

After microwaving his lunch (he hadn't yet upgraded from the cheapest brand of frozen lasagna) he'd sat in his office and resisted the urge to lean back and put his feet up on his new desk. Maybe he'd do it after everybody else left for the day.

He also had an apple and a can of root beer. He'd forgotten to put the can in the small refrigerator when he arrived here this morning, but that was okay. He didn't mind warm soda. He took the apple out of the brown paper sack and bit into it.

It was kind of soft. Not soft like a peach, but definitely

softer than a crisp, fresh apple should've been. Though it didn't taste bad, the inside was a light brownish color, like the apple had been sitting around for a couple of hours with a bite taken out of it. He looked around for his wastebasket then spat out the apple.

Wow, that grocery store really did suck. Maybe they *should* go back and say, "Hey, everything you sold us was garbage." Clearly, there were issues with their food storage.

He was surprised that Adeline had bought the apples in the first place. With milk, all you'd do is check the date; she obviously wouldn't break the seal on the jug and open it up to smell if it was spoiled or not. The bread had been in tinted plastic wrap that would've hidden the moldy parts unless you did a thorough inspection. But she'd purchased the apples individually, not in a bag, and she would've made sure to pick the best ones. She wouldn't have bought apples that were soft to the touch.

It wasn't a big deal. Just a bit weird.

CHAPTER SEVEN
BEFORE

Maddox, Fletcher, and Heck sat in the car. They were several miles from the scene of the crime, and as far as Maddox could tell they'd completely gotten away with it. Normally this was when they'd be having a few celebratory drinks, or, if that didn't seem smart, going their own ways. Instead, they'd been sitting in the car for almost ten minutes, not speaking.

Well, somebody had to break the silence. "Fuck," said Maddox.

Nobody responded.

It had gone exactly according to plan. Heck had popped the lock on the front door, and the three of them quietly went inside. The lady did indeed have a tiny yappy dog, but by the time it started barking, they were already in the bedroom. Maddox shut the dog in the closet while Fletcher and Heck held the woman down.

And then they did what they'd been paid to do.

It didn't bother Maddox how Heck had reacted. The guy was a psychopath. What bothered Maddox was how *he* had reacted. Yeah, he'd expected it to be a fun night, but he'd never imagined himself turning into a *giggling,* cackling madman.

Seriously, what the hell *was* that? The three of them were like savages. Again, that was the whole point of the job, but Maddox had assumed that they'd just be playing the role. Hack her up, splash some blood around, figure out something "funny" to do with her corpse, and be done with it.

They'd stayed in the house for almost two hours. Two hours! That was an insane risk. They should've been in there for ten minutes at the absolute most, but they simply didn't want to leave. They were having too much of a thrill behaving like lunatics who'd gone off their meds.

Heck had indeed tried to drag the lady into a private room. When Maddox had told him to knock that shit off, it wasn't out of any sense of decency. It was because he didn't want Heck having fun without him. Maddox had done far worse things to her than he'd ever envisioned Heck doing, and he did them right out there in the open, with Heck and Fletcher watching and laughing and cheering him on.

The thing was, the whole time Maddox kept thinking about how he shouldn't be behaving like this, and the thought amused him, made it even more fun, like he was getting off on being oh so very naughty. He was like a little kid who says a bad word just because he knows it's not allowed.

And then, when they were finished with the lady, when there was nothing more they could possibly do to her, Heck pointed to the closet where Maddox had put the dog and winked. Instead of punching him in the face, Maddox grinned and agreed that it was a fine way to keep the party going.

When they were finally done, they'd left the house silently, but as soon as they were back in the car they'd started whooping and laughing like drunken college students on spring break.

It took them a while to calm down. Fletcher was the first one to chill out, though since he was always the quiet one Maddox didn't really notice. The impact of what they'd done didn't hit him until they were stopped at a red light and he noticed a tuft of fur stuck in his shoelaces.

It was dark in the car and he couldn't even really see his shoes, but it didn't matter if the fur was imaginary or not. Maddox felt like total garbage.

They'd pulled into the parking lot of a twenty-four hour diner and just sat there.

"Did what we had to do," said Heck.

"Not like that."

"Exactly like that. This wasn't supposed to be a quick hit job. We knew what was going to happen." Heck looked pale, though it could've been the light.

"Like that? That's how you envisioned it?"

"More or less."

"Bullshit."

Heck sighed. "So it got out of control. There was the scent of blood in the air. Who cares if we went feral?"

"I don't like that we took such a big risk. We weren't smart about this job. Not at all."

"I agree with you. We got so caught up in what we were doing that we stopped being cautious. It could have bitten us on the ass. But it didn't."

"You look like you're gonna throw up," said Maddox.

"I have no regrets. I don't need you judging me."

"I'm judging all three of us."

"Well, if you're going to have yourself a dark night of the soul leave me out of it. Are we just going to sit here or are we going inside to get something to eat?"

"You could eat?" Maddox asked.

"I bit off one of her fingers. I think I can stomach a burger."

"Feel free to go in and have a great big ol' feast if you want. Sorry if I have no appetite. Go on. I'll see you tomorrow."

"Nah," said Heck. "I guess I'm not hungry."

"Want me to drop you off at Veronica's?"

Heck shook his head. "Not horny, either."

"I wasn't thinking she'd do you at three in the morning."

"She'll do me anytime. Just take me home."

"Let's swing by a liquor store," said Fletcher from the back seat.

"No way," said Maddox. "Nobody gets wasted."

"What do you think I'll do, confess to my fuckin' pillow?"

"We were already stupid tonight. Let's not add to it."

"Whatever."

"Real mature." Maddox turned on the engine and backed out of the parking space.

"Bitch got what was coming to her," said Heck. "Anybody who paints their house bright pink like that deserves to die."

\- - -

Edwin smiled and waved as Maddox walked into the bar. Maddox had spent all night tossing and turning and spitting up bile, and was in no mood to deal with this kid.

He sat down across from him in the booth.

"*Damn*," Edwin said.

"Just give me the money."

"I hear you guys went above and beyond. Cleanup crew had their work cut out for them. If I were the one signing your paycheck, I'd give you a bonus."

"I didn't get a second of sleep, so is there any chance we could skip the small talk?"

"Where's your sack?"

"What sack?"

"That bag thing. I can't remember the name. Starts with a C."

"Colostomy bag."

"Yeah."

"It was fake. I kept a goddamn knife in it."

"For real?"

"Yeah."

"So was that, like, effective, or just your own private little joke?"

"I never had cause to stab somebody in the throat, so I can't yet say if it was effective or not. But I'm getting close to that point with you."

Edwin held up his hands. "Whoa, dude, somebody's kind of cranky, huh? I'd never rip you off, but until you actually have your money, it seems like you'd want to be polite."

"Are you threatening me?"

"In what universe did that sound like a threat?"

"How about you give me my money before I rip your throat out with my fingernails?"

"The next time my boss has a job, I'm pretty sure you won't get a call."

"The next time your boss has a job, tell him to shove it

up his ass."

Edwin was silent for a moment, then smirked. "I'll cut you some slack because your eyes look all haunted."

"Thank you."

"I guess decorating the walls and ceiling with an old woman changes you. I can respect that you're having a tough time of it. I *am* going to say that maybe you should change the way you're talking to me, because right now I'd have to bring back a bad report. And that doesn't just impact future jobs." Edwin took a sip of his beer. "See, *now* I'm threatening you. It's easy to tell the difference because I'm not smiling anymore."

"All right, I'm sorry," said Maddox, embarrassed by the way his voice almost cracked. "It was a lot uglier than I expected. It's not sitting well with me."

"Good. That kind of thing should disturb you. Otherwise you're a sociopath." Edwin glanced around the bar, then set an envelope on the table, which Maddox quickly scooped into his lap. "It's all there. If you want to go out to your car and count it, I'll be here until I finish my beer."

"I trust you," said Maddox, sliding out of the booth. "Sorry again."

- - -

Maddox didn't need to check himself in the mirror to know how bad he looked. He'd only been sleeping an hour or two a night for the past week. Couldn't keep food down. Didn't want to talk to anybody. Wasn't even able to maintain enough focus to watch mindless TV shows.

Weirdly, he wasn't at all worried about being caught.

He should've been. Five minutes in, they'd stopped even pretending to be cautious. Heck, at least, had left DNA all over the damn place. But Maddox wasn't concerned. Even when he lay in bed and specifically thought to himself, *my partner left DNA evidence all over the scene of a murder,* it didn't bother him. The only thing to consume him was the shame and the guilt.

Why wasn't it the other way around? He didn't give a shit about that lady. Maybe she deserved it, maybe she didn't, but he'd killed people before—including at least one guy that he knew for certain didn't deserve it—without his conscience bugging him. Yet he'd often replay the details of his various crimes in his mind, trying to figure out where he might have slipped up in a way that could lead the cops to him. It was like his brain had been rewired.

His phone rang. It took him a moment to find it between the couch cushions. When he dug it out, he saw that it was Fletcher. "Yeah?"

"Hey."

"Hey."

Fletcher let out a long sigh. "We shouldn't have done that."

"No shit, you think?"

"We have to make it right."

"Yeah," said Maddox. "We really do."

Maddox was completely aware of how stupid they sounded. Make it right? What were they going to do, scoop the pieces of the woman together and apologize to the pile? Turn themselves in to the cops? Kill themselves?

"I want to give the money back," said Fletcher. "I already talked to Heck and he agrees with me."

Maddox nodded, even though Fletcher couldn't see him.

"I'm totally on board with that. I don't know if it'll clear my conscience, but it's worth a shot. It's the right thing to do. We'll bring it to the house on Stanford, right?"

Despite what he was saying, Maddox was not completely on board with that. Giving back the money would not clear his conscience and was not the right thing to do. He'd never heard of the house on Stanford. Part of his mind kept saying *What the fuck are you talking about?* while another part of his mind thought it all sounded completely rational. Bring the money to the house on Stanford. Of course. That would make all of his problems disappear.

"I'm so glad you agree with us," said Fletcher, sounding almost tearful with relief.

"We're in this together."

"When do you want to do it?"

"As soon as possible. Are you free now?" Suddenly a better idea occurred to Maddox. "No, wait, now is not the right time. After dark. We should do it as soon as possible after dark."

"After dark, yes," said Fletcher. "That's exactly what I was thinking."

"Good. We're in this together. I'll pick you guys up around seven."

"Perfect. I already spent some of the money, but I'm gonna sell some shit to make sure I've got my share. We'll get through this, man."

"Yeah, we will. A lot of guys would turn on each other when things got bad like this, but not us. We're sticking together. We're fuckin' brothers."

"Brothers."

"It's gonna be fine. We're gonna do the right thing."

CHAPTER EIGHT

T he optometrist was the hairiest human being Adeline had ever seen. She wanted to ask him if this meant that werewolves had perfect vision, but she'd just met him and wasn't sure how he'd respond to the joke.

"Contact lenses can take a little while to get used to," Dr. Velasco told Paige. "But you'll get the hang of putting them in, I promise."

Paige nodded.

"The first thing you'll always do is wash your hands. You don't want anything going from your fingers to the lens and then onto your eye."

Paige turned on the faucet, squirted some soap onto her hands, and washed them thoroughly.

"It's best to dry them with a lint-free cloth," said Dr. Velasco. "Otherwise you get specks of lint in your eyes, and you don't want that, right?"

"Nope," said Paige.

After Paige dried her hands, Dr. Velasco gave her one of the lens packets. "Tear this open and put the lens on your index finger. You'll want to make sure it's not inside out, so what you'll look for are the numbers 1-2-3 on the side. If they're upside-down, the lens is the wrong way."

"What happens if I put it in the wrong way?" Paige asked.

"It'll be uncomfortable. You'll feel that it's wrong, but it's better to figure that out before you actually put it on your eye. Do you see the numbers?"

"It's hard to see them without my glasses."

Dr. Velasco chuckled. "Yeah, that's kind of a Catch-22, isn't it? You need to be able to see the numbers to put in the contacts that let you see."

"Okay, I see it. 1-2-3."

Adeline watched as the optometrist talked Paige through the process of actually placing the contact lens on her eyeball. Paige kept blinking, causing the lens to fold up.

"Don't get frustrated," said Dr. Velasco. "I've been through this with lots and lots of people. You're doing better than you think you are. We're used to purposely *not* touching our eyes, so this doesn't come naturally to anybody. It just takes practice. I've seen people your mom's age do a lot worse than you."

"Your mom's age" was clearly not meant to be an insult—Dr. Velasco looked to be in his fifties—but Adeline was suddenly less inclined to worry about offending him with a werewolf joke.

On the ninth or tenth try, Paige successfully got the lens onto her right eye. The left lens only took four tries.

"See? Easier already," said Dr. Velasco.

Paige blinked a few times then looked at herself in the mirror.

"What do you think?" Adeline asked.

"I love them."

"Excellent," said Dr. Velasco. "You can sleep with

them in, but I recommend you take them out every night until you get used to them. It's good to get in the practice of putting them in and taking them out. Speaking of which, let's take them out. What you're going to do is look up, then use your thumb and index finger, and pinch."

"Pinch?" asked Paige, sounding unsure.

Dr. Velasco chuckled. "You'll get used to it, I promise."

- - -

"Well, who is *that* stunning lady?" asked Boyd when he came home from work.

"Do they look cool?" asked Paige, opening her eyes comically wide.

"They look great. How do they feel?"

"I can't really tell they're in."

"Good. It's nice. I can see your eyes better."

After Paige went into her room, Boyd and Adeline sat down on the living room sofa. "How was your day?" Adeline asked.

"Tiring. I definitely have more respect for what Mr. Prace went through." He put his arm around her. "I never thought Paige looked bad with glasses. I'm not sure why she wanted to get rid of them."

"I don't think she wants to look better. I think she wants to look different."

"Ah, okay. That makes sense."

"Be ready for her to ask to color her hair."

"I'm okay with that," said Boyd.

"Liar."

"Depends on the color, I guess."

"What color would bother you?"

Boyd considered that. "I'm not sure. These days there really isn't any color that's considered particularly strange. Maybe if she went gray so that she looked like an old lady. I suppose blue or green or red would be fine. I mean, I wouldn't encourage it, I hope she sticks with blonde, but I wouldn't try to forbid a color change. It might be that I'm more worried about a really weird hairstyle."

"Like a Mohawk?"

"Yeah. Mohawks are fine for the right person, but I don't think it suits her head shape." Boyd coughed.

"You okay?" Adeline asked.

He coughed again. "Yeah, yeah, I'm fine."

"I hope you and Naomi aren't coming down with something."

"I hope so, too. I don't feel sick, though." He coughed once more, and then got up off the couch. "I'm going to get a drink of water."

Adeline followed him into the kitchen. Boyd took down a glass and filled it from the faucet. He frowned before he took a drink.

"What's wrong?" Adeline asked.

"What's the deal with the bananas?"

Adeline glanced over at the counter. The bananas had turned completely brown.

"Oh my God. I just bought those today and they were weren't even ripe yet. They were green. How did that happen?"

"I forgot to say anything, but the apple you packed me for lunch was rotten inside, too."

"I went to a different grocery store. There was nothing wrong with the apples when I bought them. I checked.

What would make this happen?"

"I don't know," said Boyd. "Something in the air, maybe?"

"What in the air? Apples don't rot like that."

"Heat, maybe? A vent that was pointing right at them?"

"The milk was in the refrigerator."

"Then honestly I have no idea. I don't know what would make food go bad. We could go over and see if our neighbors are having the same problem."

Adeline smiled. "'Hello, we're the Gardners. By any chance is your fruit rotting at a freakishly accelerated speed?'"

"I've never heard of that kind of thing happening. Maybe local crops are bad or something? That wouldn't explain the milk and bread. Could a whole supplier have been impacted? That doesn't seem likely. I mean, if their refrigeration system failed, the bananas would've been brown before you bought them."

"Yeah. Like I said, they weren't ripe enough to eat this morning."

"It feels like we're spending way too much time discussing spoiled fruit, but it's odd, don't you think?"

Adeline nodded. "Odd as hell."

"If it keeps happening, we'll call somebody over to check things out."

"Who would we call?"

"No clue." Boyd coughed. "Damn, I hope I'm not getting sick. I can't stay home from work my first week, and I don't want to infect everybody there and have *them* call in sick."

"You should load up on Vitamin C and go to bed early."

"Yeah, that's probably a good idea."

- - -

Adeline was not surprised that Boyd didn't go to bed early. "I should go to bed early," was a common refrain in their household, one often uttered but rarely fulfilled. He didn't cough again—at least not that Adeline noticed—and insisted that he felt totally fine.

"Are you ready to take your contacts out?" Adeline asked Paige.

"Yep."

"Want me to help?"

"How would you help?"

"I guess I meant watch."

"Why would I want you to watch?"

"I'm trying to be a supportive mother."

"If you want to stare at me creepily while I take out my contacts, be my guest."

"You know what? I'm going to do exactly that. Let's go."

They walked to the bathroom. Adeline stood in the doorway while Paige looked at herself in the mirror. She held her thumb and index finger up to her right eye, pinched, and missed.

"You're supposed to look up," said Adeline.

"I know."

"You didn't look up."

Paige looked up, pinched, and missed again.

"It's hard."

"That's because you're not used to sticking fingers in your eye."

"It's not as squishy as I thought it would be."

"If you can tell if your eye is squishy or not, you're pressing too hard."

"I can't do this while you're talking."

Adeline shut up. Paige looked up. Pinched. Missed.

"Dammit."

"Paige!"

"I can't get it."

"That's no reason for that kind of language."

"I think I'm old enough to say dammit."

"I think you're not."

"Whatever. Fudge, then."

"I'll just leave you alone."

"Thanks, Mom."

Adeline walked back into the living room.

"I liked Paige better with glasses," said Naomi.

"Well, promise me you won't tell her that."

"I won't. Can I get my nose pierced?"

"Um, how about we start with your ears, honey?"

"Okay." Naomi grinned. "Paige told me to ask about my nose first so you'd say yes to my ears."

"Your sister is very clever."

Several minutes later, Paige stepped into the living room. Her eyes were red.

"Got 'em out," she said.

"It'll get easier. It's only day one."

"Yep. I still like them."

- - -

Adeline lay next to Boyd in bed, both of them reading. She set her book on the nightstand and gently ran her hand over his thigh.

"Yes," she said. "I'm a bit horny. I assume that doesn't

disappoint you?"

Boyd set his own book down. "Actually, I've kind of got a headache."

"Oh. All right. Do you want me to get you some aspirin?"

"I took some. It's not helping."

"Well...okay."

"It's nothing major," said Boyd. "I just don't feel all that great."

Adeline could only think of two times during their entire marriage that Boyd had declined sex: once while they were visiting his parents, and once while they were in an empty movie theater. (The movie theater had been a good call, since somebody came in less than a minute after Boyd rejected her advance.) He'd once tried to initiate sex when he had a 103-degree fever.

"It's all right," said Adeline.

"I mean, if you're really horny—"

"Nope. Just a bit."

"I can try."

"It's all good."

"You could pull out the toy box."

"I am one hundred percent fine. This was really more for your benefit. I didn't know you still weren't feeling well."

"I'm sure it's no big deal. It's not like I'm dying or anything. Just a little under the weather."

"Anything I can do?"

"Nah, I'll be fine in the morning."

Adeline shut off the light. Actually, the toy box *was* tempting, but no, those were meant for special occasions, not to compensate for a sick husband.

Usually they snuggled for a while before they fell

asleep, but she didn't want to catch any germs, so she rolled on her side, facing away from him, and closed her eyes.

A few minutes later there was a knock at the door.

"Mommy?" asked Naomi from outside.

Adeline reached over and turned the light back on. "Yes, sweetie? Is everything okay?"

"Gordon got out of his aquarium."

CHAPTER NINE

*B*oyd sat up. "What the fuck did she say?" he whispered to Adeline.

"Shhh."

"What do you mean he got out of his aquarium?" Boyd called out.

"He's not in there."

Boyd turned on the light and got out of bed. He hurried over to the door and opened it. Naomi stood there in her nightgown, looking worried. Boyd knelt down in front of her.

"Where is he?"

"I don't know."

"How long has he been out?"

"I don't know."

"When was the last time you saw him?"

"I don't know."

"Yes, you do."

"Before dinner."

"So he could've been on the loose for three hours?"

Naomi didn't respond.

"Go look for him," Boyd said. "I'll be there in a minute to help."

Naomi left. Boyd put on a pair of slippers. Then he decided that the slippers didn't offer sufficient protection, took them off, and began to put on a pair of shoes.

"You don't have to help look," said Adeline.

"Yes, I do. I'm her father."

"The rest of us can look. You can stay here."

"I'm not going to be a chickenshit," said Boyd, tying the laces. "But do you see now that a tarantula is not a viable pet? We've got a goddamn giant spider crawling around our new home. That's not okay. That's really not okay."

"Nobody will think less of you if you don't help search," Adeline insisted.

Boyd wanted to take her up on that offer, but, no, he couldn't let his daughters see his cowardice. They were getting rid of that spider after it was found, though. Pet shop, abandoned deep in the forest...Boyd didn't care, but Gordon's reign of terror in this household was over.

Stupid frickin' spider. Eight-legged piece of crap. It had better hope that Boyd didn't find its ass next to a can of Raid.

Boyd finished tying his shoes, and he and Adeline left the bedroom. As they walked toward Naomi's room, Paige stepped out of her own bedroom.

"What's wrong?" she asked, rubbing her eyes.

"Gordon escaped," Boyd told her.

"Uh-oh."

"Uh-oh is right. So watch where you step."

"I'll help look."

Boyd went into Naomi's bedroom. The lid of the aquarium was open.

"So you left the lid open?" Boyd asked.

"I don't remember."

"Had you opened the lid earlier?"

"Yes. I was feeding him."

"So, even though I've said repeatedly that you are *never* to leave the lid open when you're not actively watching Gordon, it's possible that you left the lid open when you weren't in your room?"

Naomi looked at the floor. "Yes."

"This is what we can expect from you having your own bedroom, huh? Do we need to move you back in with your sister?"

"No!"

"We'll discuss this after we find the little creep. Start looking."

Boyd hated to play the role of the Angry Dad, but this was exactly why he didn't want her to have a tarantula in the first place. What if they never found it? What if he had to spend the entire next year stressing about when and where it would finally turn up? He wouldn't even be able to take a dump in peace without imagining that the spider was lurking on the underside of the toilet lid.

Naomi looked around the floor. Adeline checked the walls. Boyd got down on his hands and knees and peeked under the dresser.

He couldn't see anything. It was too dark under there.

"Adeline, do you know if we ever unpacked the flashlight?"

"I don't think so."

"Of course not. Do you know which box it's in?"

"There are a few possibilities."

"Well, could you *look*?" he asked.

"Sure."

"No, wait, I'm sorry." He was being a jerk. Even

though there was a big hairy tarantula free in his home, there was no reason to be unpleasant to his family. That was never acceptable. "That tone wasn't appropriate. I apologize."

"I think I know which box it's in," said Adeline. "It's in the basement. Back in a minute."

Adeline left.

"Will Gordon be okay?" Naomi asked.

"It depends who finds him."

Naomi sniffled.

"Gordon will be fine," said Boyd. "Do you remember if you left your door open or not?"

"I'm not sure."

"Think, honey."

"I think..." Naomi furrowed her brow in deep concentration. "...I left it open."

"Well, sure, that's the answer I expected." Boyd closed his eyes and took a deep, calming breath. "We'll just search room by room, and we'll close off each room after we're done. We know he's still in the house. We'll find him."

"Promise?" Naomi asked, looking up at him with her big eyes, her lips trembling as she fought back tears.

This could be a promise that blew up in his face, since for all Boyd knew a book had fallen off a shelf and crushed the damn thing. And if he promised Naomi that they'd find her beloved pet unharmed, it would make things more difficult when he told her she had to get rid of it. Naomi was only eight years old. He didn't want to say, "You may be personally responsible for Gordon's untimely death."

"Just keep looking," he said, hoping Naomi wouldn't insist on a promise. "He's not on the walls and he's not on the floor that we can see." Boyd looked up, half expecting the tarantula to drop from the ceiling, land on his face, and scurry into his open mouth. "He's not on the ceiling. Check your blankets to make sure he didn't crawl under them."

Whether they found the spider or not, Boyd was going to have nightmares about tarantulas squirming under his blankets.

Adeline stepped into the bedroom, holding the flashlight. "Found it in the first box I checked."

"Thanks," said Boyd, taking the flashlight from her. He got back down on the floor and shined the beam underneath Naomi's dresser. Somehow there were already a couple of dirty socks under there. No tarantula that he could see. Though he couldn't see everything, and there were some corners where it could hide...

Boyd stood up. "I don't think it's under there," he told Naomi, "but I can't see the front edges. Just sweep your hand on each side. Carefully, so you don't squish him if he's under there."

Naomi shook her head.

"What's wrong?" Boyd asked.

"I'm scared."

"Of what?"

"Gordon."

"What do you mean, you're scared of him? He's your pet! I've seen you reach into the aquarium and touch him lots of times!"

"I can see him then."

Boyd supposed he could see her point. He certainly wasn't going to stand there and try to convince his daughter that she shouldn't be scared to reach into the darkness where a tarantula might lurk.

"Adeline?" he asked.

"Nope. No way."

"Well, I will let that thing starve to death before I so much as stick a pinky finger under that dresser. I guess we'll worry about that after we check under the bed." He should have checked under the bed before he got up off the floor in the first place, but his arachnophobia was impairing his decision making process.

Boyd crouched back down and aimed the flashlight beam under the bed.

"Seriously, Naomi, why is there so much junk under here? We just moved here! Shouldn't this stuff accumulate instead of being thrown under there all at once?"

"Do you see Gordon?" Naomi asked, ignoring his question.

"There are a million places for him to hide. I'm not reaching under there to move anything." He sat up. "We'll lift up your mattress and see if we can find him. If we can't, we'll have to use a stick or something to get this garbage out of the way. But I mean it, Naomi, this mess is ridiculous."

"I don't like things clean. It makes my room less fun."

Boyd picked up one end of the mattress and Adeline took the other. They lifted it off the box springs.

"Is he there?" Adeline asked Naomi.

Naomi looked for a few moments. "Ummm..."

"Take your time," said Boyd, who knew he shouldn't be sarcastic toward his young daughter.

"Move your head," said Adeline. "We need to put the mattress down, quick."

"Are your arms giving out?" Boyd asked.

"No, can't you hear Paige crying?"

Boyd listened. Yes, Paige was crying in another room. They set the mattress down and hurried out of Naomi's room and down the hallway. Paige stood in the bathroom, staring in the mirror, tears streaming down her cheeks.

"What's wrong?" asked Adeline.

"I was putting in my contacts so I could help look for Gordon," said Paige, stuttering and sniffling. "It went back up in my eye. I can't find it."

Adeline put her hands on Paige's shoulders and peered at her. "Open your eyes wider. Good. So you're sure it's still in there?"

Paige nodded. "I can feel it."

Adeline moved her face closer to Paige's. "I don't see it. Boyd, do you still have the flashlight?"

"No, I'll be back." Boyd returned to Naomi's room and picked up the flashlight.

"Is Paige okay?" Naomi asked.

"Yeah, she's fine. Don't worry. Keep looking for Gordon."

Boyd went back to the bathroom and gave Adeline the flashlight. She shone the beam directly into Paige's right eye. "I still don't see it."

"It's in there."

"Push up your eyelid."

Paige did so. Boyd was no fan of eye-related stuff, but since everybody in the house knew of his fear of spiders, he wasn't going to admit to cringing here.

"I still can't see it," said Adeline. "It must be way back there."

"It's okay, honey," Boyd assured Paige. "It can't get lost."

He hoped that was true. Could a contact slip so far

back onto your eye that you couldn't get it out? He'd never heard of such a thing, but he was also not an inexhaustible resource of horrific anecdotes from contact lens wearers. "Contact lens goes all the way to the back of your eyeball" seemed like something that would be an urban legend, not a legitimate risk.

"Could you get me a tissue?" Adeline asked Boyd.

He unrolled some toilet paper and handed it to her. Adeline wiped snot off Paige's face, and then handed the gooey tissue back to Boyd.

"Breathe, sweetie," said Adeline. "I promise you we'll get it out. I need you to stay calm and still, okay?"

Paige nodded.

"So you can feel it on your eye, but you can't feel it with your fingers, right?"

"Right."

"Okay. I'm going to see if I can feel it. I'll be gentle. Close your eyes."

Paige closed her eyes. Adeline placed her index and middle finger on Paige's eyelid and slid her fingers around.

"Anything?" asked Boyd.

"No."

"Should we take her to the emergency room?"

"Not yet."

"What if it—?" Boyd was going to ask, "What if it gets imbedded in her eye?" but he didn't want to ask that question in front of a scared little girl.

"It's going to be totally fine," Adeline assured her. "There's absolutely nothing for you to worry about. I'll get it out for you."

"Okay," said Paige, not sounding convinced.

"You're sure it's at the top, right?"

"Yes."

"I'm going to lift your eyelid. If it hurts, let me know and I'll stop, all right?"

"What's wrong with Paige?" asked Naomi, stepping into the doorway.

"Shhhh," said Boyd. "She's fine. Let Mom take care of her."

Adeline handed the flashlight to Boyd. "Can you point this at her eye for me?"

"Sure." Boyd aimed the beam. Adeline pushed Paige's eyelid back, then used her thumb to lift it a bit.

Paige whimpered.

"Try not to blink," Adeline told her.

Boyd wanted to look away, and then felt like a terrible father for that thought. It was uncomfortable to watch, but it wasn't like open-heart surgery. He could handle being a bit creeped out.

"Not seeing it yet," said Adeline.

Boyd wished he had a better understanding of eye anatomy. He couldn't imagine that a contact lens sliding up on somebody's eye could require surgery to remove, but...

He needed to stop thinking of scenarios like that. Adeline would get it out, no problem.

Adeline lifted Paige's eyelid a bit more. "Angle the light better so I can see underneath it," she told Boyd. He adjusted the flashlight beam. "Yeah, just like that...okay, I think I see it..."

Naomi stepped forward for a closer look. Boyd tugged on the collar of her nightgown to pull her back.

Adeline removed her fingers from Paige's eyelid. "I saw the edge of it. I can't go sticking my finger into your eye, and I'm definitely not going to use tweezers or anything. All we're going to do is very gently massage your eyelid and see if we can work it down far enough that I can get it out."

"Should you be rubbing her eyes?" asked Boyd. "Can't that cause damage?"

"Do you have a better idea?"

"Naomi, go get my phone. It's on the stand on my side of the bed."

Naomi rushed off, visibly pleased to have a mission.

"I'm going to look it up," he said. "That's what the Internet is for." When Naomi returned, Boyd did a quick search for *Contact lens lost in eye* and read the first article that popped up. "So, first of all, it can't get permanently lost," he reported. "There's a membrane around your eye to keep that from happening. What we're going to do is give you some eye drops, and then you're going to look down and keep blinking."

Adeline held Paige's eye open while she applied the wetting drops, a process that Paige did not enjoy.

"Just blink," said Boyd. "It'll come out. Don't worry."

Paige wiped tears from her cheeks and stood there, looking down and blinking.

After about a minute, Adeline asked, "Does it feel any different?"

"Not really."

"Put in some more drops," Boyd said.

"I can do it," said Paige, taking the tiny plastic bottle from Adeline. She tilted her head back, held her eye open with her left hand, and put in the drops with her right, flinching each time a drop hit her eyeball. She looked down and resumed the blinking process.

Everybody stood there, trying to wait patiently for the eye drops to do the trick.

"Did it come out?" asked Paige.

"I didn't see it," Adeline told her.

"I can't feel it anymore."

"I didn't see it come out, either," said Boyd.

Paige rubbed her eyelid. "Maybe it didn't."

"But it feels okay now?" asked Adeline.

"Yeah. I could feel it in there before but now I can't."

"I hope it didn't slide so far back that you can't feel it," said Adeline.

"There's no reason it would have moved further back," said Boyd. "Maybe it *did* drop out." He crouched down and shined the flashlight on the tile floor by her feet. No sign of the contact lens.

"Did it fall under your nightgown?" asked Adeline.

"I'm not going to check with you guys standing here."

"Fine," said Boyd. "See if you can find it." He was pretty sure that he, Adeline, and Naomi wouldn't have missed a contact lens falling out of her eye, but there were a lot of tears and the lens was transparent, so he supposed that it was possible.

Paige closed the bathroom door as everybody else stepped out into the hallway.

"Well, that was exciting," said Adeline.

"Yeah, a fun-filled roller coaster."

"I think we can postpone the Gordon search until tomorrow."

"You're kidding, right?" Boyd asked.

"Don't you think you should get some sleep? You've got work in the morning. We'll find him."

"No, no, no, no, no, no. There is no way in hell I'm going to bed until that thing is accounted for. I'm not going to wake up to that thing crawling on my toes."

"Our bedroom door will be shut."

"What if it's already in there?"

"I'm sure it's not."

"That's not good enough. I'm sorry, but when it comes to tarantulas on my toes, I don't take any chances. Just no."

The bathroom door opened. "I can't find it anywhere," said Paige.

"You don't think it could still be in your eye?" asked Boyd.

Paige shrugged. "It could be. I don't think it is. Before I felt it every time I blinked, and I don't anymore."

"It wouldn't just disappear, though." Boyd had an image of the contact lens burrowing into her eye. An absurd image, of course, but one that was kind of unsettling.

"Should we take her to the hospital?" asked Adeline.

Boyd sighed. "I don't know. It doesn't seem like that should be necessary, but I also don't want to wake up tomorrow and find out that she scratched her cornea."

"I don't want to scratch my cornea," said Paige.

"I'll take her in," said Boyd. "You and Naomi keep looking for that stupid spider."

CHAPTER TEN

Paige seemed fairly relaxed as Boyd sat with her in the hospital waiting room. More relaxed than he would be if he had a contact lens possibly lost deep in his eyeball socket. He was pretty sure this was just a precautionary measure, but better to be safe than to discover that the lens was indeed sliding around in there doing damage.

And, though he'd never admit this to anybody, he'd rather be at a hospital than at home searching for that goddamn tarantula.

"If you want to go back to glasses, that's all right," Boyd told her. "Your mom and I won't be mad."

"It's only one bad experience," Paige said, her tone of voice indicating that he was a silly father who was unaware of his daughter's high maturity level. "I'm sure I just put them in wrong."

"Fair enough. I wanted to make it clear that just because we paid for new contacts doesn't mean you have to wear them." That actually sounded kind of passive-aggressive. As he had many times in the past while having conversations with his daughters, Boyd decided to let it drop.

\- \- \-

Adeline was not particularly frightened of Gordon. Unlike Boyd, she didn't mind having the spider in the house. She didn't think there was anything wrong with Naomi having him for a pet. She would've been able to get a good night's sleep knowing that he was out of his aquarium.

That did *not* mean that she was willing to reach underneath Naomi's bed searching for the tarantula.

They'd been using a broom handle to carefully slide things out from under the bed (while continuing the "maybe you should be less of a slob" lecture). Adeline had a mild sense of dread with each new item, thinking that this could be the one with a crushed spider stuck to it.

"What if he got out of the house?" Naomi asked.

"I don't see how he could," said Adeline. "Even with eight legs he couldn't open a door."

Naomi was not amused by her joke.

"There's nowhere for him to go," Adeline continued. "He's too big to squeeze under a door or get through the air conditioning vent. Unless there's a hole in the floor that nobody noticed, he's still in the house."

"Okay."

Adeline used the broom to move a shoebox. Something was behind it that might have been tarantula-shaped, but it was too dark to tell for sure. She picked up the flashlight.

"Aw, shit."

- - -

Boyd sat on a chair in the examination room while the doctor shined a penlight into Paige's eye.

His cell phone vibrated. A text from Adeline.

Gordon dead. Naomi inconsolable. How's YOUR night going?

Oh shit, Boyd texted back.

Yep.

Where was he?

Under the bed.

Squashed?

You'll need to see it.

??????

You'll see when you get home. How's Paige?

"I don't see any sign of a foreign object lodged in there," said the doctor, sounding almost disappointed.

"You don't think we'd need an X-Ray or something?" asked Boyd.

"Oh, no. A contact lens wouldn't show up in an X-Ray. An MRI, maybe, but there's absolutely no reason that we'd take that step. There's honestly not much room in your eye for something to hide. Even if it were in there, I'd tell you not to worry; it would come out on its own. But it's not in there."

"Good to hear," said Boyd. "We were just worried because we didn't see it fall out and we couldn't find it on the floor."

"It's a tiny lens that's meant to look invisible."

"Still, it was a tile floor."

The doctor shrugged. "I don't know what to tell you. It's not in her eye now."

"Thank you. I appreciate it."

- - -

Boyd felt squirmy as they drove home. He knew he should be relieved, and he was, but he really hoped that the lens turned up. It was unnerving having its location be unresolved. Not that he genuinely believed it might be working its way into his daughter's brain; he simply wasn't convinced that it wasn't still lodged in there, near the very top. Perhaps it was just paranoia, but if you put something in your eye, you should have physical evidence that it was no longer in your eye.

"So," he said. "Your mom texted me while the doctor was looking at you. I've got bad news. Gordon's dead."

"Oh no. Did she accidentally step on him?"

"No."

"What happened?"

"I don't know. He was under the bed."

"Are you happy?"

"Of course not. Naomi loved him."

"But you didn't."

"No, I sure didn't. I hated that thing. Doesn't mean I want your sister to be upset. Just try to be extra nice to her when we get home, okay?"

"What did you think I would do?" asked Paige. "Get in her face and go 'Ha ha, your bug is dead!'?"

"You know what I meant, smartass."

"I'm sure Mom's telling her the same thing about my traumatic experience. We'll be so nice to each other that it'll make you both sick."

- - -

When they got home, Naomi had fallen asleep

snuggled against Adeline on the living room couch. Adeline slowly extricated herself from the cuddles without waking her up, then got up and gave Paige a hug.

"Glad everything's okay," she said.

"Yeah, my eyeball didn't get slashed apart, so that's good," said Paige. "The doctor took it out of the socket and everything. Did he put it back in straight?" Paige looked at her, cross-eyed.

"It would appear that you're feeling better," said Adeline.

"When my eyeball was out the doctor poked my brain to make me forget my fear."

"Time for you to go to bed."

"What happened to Gordon?"

Adeline looked over at Naomi, who was still asleep. "We found him dead," she whispered. "We'll talk about it tomorrow. Bedtime."

"Okay, let me put my contacts in and then I'll go to sleep."

"Ha ha. Go away."

Paige left the living room. Adeline's smile disappeared.

"So what exactly happened?" Boyd asked.

"C'mon."

She led Boyd into the kitchen. There was a closed Tupperware container next to the sink.

"I didn't want to leave him under the bed, so I scooped him up with a spatula," said Adeline, removing the lid. Boyd glanced inside.

The dead tarantula lay on its back, all eight legs folded in. Its body was covered with green and white mold.

Boyd stared at it for a moment, then stepped back, unable to shake the childish concern that the spider might spring back to life. "What the hell?"

"Doesn't it look like he rotted?"

"Yeah."

"It would be different if there'd maybe been a line of ants leading to the body. But this isn't how an insect decomposes. Why is it moldy?"

That was, Boyd had to admit, an excellent question. The quickly rotting fruit was bizarre, but this was crossing the line into flat-out disturbing. Boyd didn't know a lot about entomology (he did know that spiders weren't insects, though now was not the time to be pedantic) but what happened to that tarantula was not the natural order of things.

"I'll call Jack Ponter tomorrow and tell him exactly what's going on. He needs to send somebody over to investigate."

"Who would he send?"

"I don't know. That's his problem. There's something wrong with the air quality in this house and they need to take care of it. If they have to scrub down the entire place, attic to basement, they can put us up in a hotel."

"Maybe we should go to a hotel tonight," said Adeline. "What if we're getting poisoned?"

Boyd wanted nothing more than to just go to bed—he was only going to get about five hours of sleep as it was—and he didn't think they'd get reimbursed for the hotel room after the fact. But there was clearly something wrong with this house, and he didn't want to risk something that might have long-lasting effects on his daughters.

Adeline seemed to notice his hesitation. "I'm probably overreacting."

Boyd shook his head. "Better to play it safe. We don't want something toxic getting into our lungs. We'll find a hotel and then get Jack over here tomorrow. If you want to pack a change of clothes for Naomi, I'll pack our stuff."

"Maybe we don't need to go tonight. We'll sleep here and then I'll take the girls someplace during the day."

"Gordon is covered with mold. We should not be sleeping here tonight."

Adeline walked toward Naomi's room. Boyd went over to Paige's room and stood in her doorway. She was sitting on her bed, holding a pair of fingernail clippers.

"Pick out some clothes for tomorrow," said Boyd. "We're staying at a hotel tonight."

"Why?"

"There's mold in the house. We shouldn't be breathing it."

"Okay. Let me finish this."

"Are you clipping your fingernails in bed?"

"I'm clipping them while I'm sitting on my bed."

"Do you really want fingernail clippings on your blankets? That's gross."

"I'm watching where they go."

"Hey, it's your bed. If you want it to be covered with fingernails, that's your call. Civilized people do it in the bathroom over a waste basket."

"I guess I'm a cavewoman."

"I guess so. If you decide to make fire, promise me you'll—" Boyd frowned. "Let me see your hand."

Paige held up her left hand. Thin trickles of blood had run down three of her fingers. She seemed to notice this at the same time Boyd did.

Boyd rushed over and knelt down next to her. He took her hand in his own so he could get a better look. She'd cut her fingernails so close to the quick that they were bleeding.

"Jesus, Paige!"

Paige looked flustered. "I—I must not have been paying attention."

"Doesn't it hurt?"

"It does now."

What the hell was happening? Sure, he'd trimmed his own nail too far back before, but that was something you did on accident *once*, not to every finger.

"What made you do this?" Boyd demanded.

"I told you. I wasn't paying attention."

"You're thirteen years old. You know how to clip your fingernails. Did you do this on purpose?"

"No!" Paige seemed genuinely horrified by the idea. "It was a mistake!"

"Every finger has blood on it."

"Not that much."

"What's wrong?" Adeline asked, stepping into Paige's bedroom.

Boyd held up Paige's hand to show her.

"Oh my God. What happened?"

"I messed up, okay?" said Paige. "I was thinking about what happened to my eye and I wasn't paying attention to what I was doing. I wasn't trying to hurt myself, I promise." She began to cry.

Boyd looked at her hand once more. The skin that wasn't bleeding was raw and red. She was going to be in pain for quite a while, not counting the upcoming moment of agony when they poured on the antiseptic.

He could see one of the fingernails on her bed with a piece of flesh stuck to it.

He put his arms around his daughter and gave her a tight hug as she sobbed into his chest.

To hell with this house.

CHAPTER ELEVEN

The closest motel was a few miles away. It sucked.

There were rust stains in the shower and discolored water in the toilet. The towels were so threadbare that if an auto mechanic used them to wipe up oil spills, he'd secretly think, "I can do better." The room reeked of marijuana, forcing Boyd and Adeline to come up with a cover story about the untimely demise of a skunk on the premises. Boyd was pretty sure that the housekeeper hadn't changed the sheets after the previous occupant, since there were still potato chip crumbs on them.

They definitely would not be staying in this place for more than one night. For now, though, Boyd just wanted to lay safely on top of the covers and go to sleep.

- - -

The next morning, Adeline was so psyched up to do battle with the landlord that it was almost a letdown when Jack Ponter apologized profusely and promised to send a cleaning crew to the house that day.

"I swear we had a crew out there before you moved

in," he told her over the phone. "I must not have done a good enough inspection after they were finished. We'll vacuum out the air ducts again and I'll get somebody in there to check for mold. We'll make sure it's a safe environment for your kids."

Adeline checked out of the motel and took the girls out for a nice breakfast of strawberry covered waffles for her and Paige and chocolate-chip pancakes for Naomi. They made a quick stop at the grocery and then returned to the house to meet Jack at ten.

"Sorry again about this," he said. "I really can't explain it."

"It's okay," Adeline assured him as she let him inside. "The house *looks* totally clean. Boyd and I certainly didn't notice anything wrong while we were moving in."

"Let me make sure I understand. Boyd said that food keeps spoiling?"

"Right. Wait here for a moment." Adeline left the house and walked to the car. She opened the passenger-side door, picked up the banana that was resting on the seat, and returned to the house. "We're going to do a weird banana experiment."

"Okay," said Jack, sounding uncertain.

She led him to the kitchen and then handed him the banana. "Not ripe yet, correct?"

"Correct."

"Still completely green?"

"Yep, green all over. Is this a magic trick?"

"I wish." Adeline took the banana from him and set it on the counter. "It's going to turn black."

"Before my very eyes?"

Adeline smiled. "Not quite that fast. But you'll be amazed. Just check on it every once in a while."

"I will," said Jack. "I'm not going to be here the whole day, but I'll make sure that nobody touches or eats it."

"If I had an extra phone, I'd set it up and record the whole thing," said Adeline. "Maybe the scientific community would be interested."

"I have to admit, I've never heard of this kind of thing happening. But we'll figure out the problem and make it stop. The cleaners should get here around ten-thirty, and I'll poke around myself until then. You're welcome to stick around here or find a more interesting way to spend your day."

"I think the girls and I are going to catch a double-feature."

"Great idea."

"Hi," said Paige, stepping into the kitchen.

"Hello, young lady," said Jack. "I'm Jack. Nice to meet you."

"Nice to meet you, too. I'm Paige." She was capable of being extremely polite when she was so inclined. Adeline was ninety-nine percent sure that it wasn't sarcasm.

Jack glanced at the bandages covering each finger on her left hand. "Did you burn yourself?" he asked.

Paige shook her head. "It was a stupid accident. I feel like a total jerk."

Adeline hoped that Jack didn't press for more details. Though she wanted him to know that there was something seriously wrong with this house, Paige's "accident" was none of his business. It wasn't as if she could really blame the house anyway. Mold didn't cause teenaged girls to—well, Adeline wouldn't go so far as to call it self-mutilation. She wasn't sure what she'd call it. Extreme carelessness brought about by an unhealthy environment. It didn't matter what she called it or what caused it; Paige hurting herself was none of Jack's concern.

"Well, remind me to tell you about how I broke my foot in college," said Jack. "Now *that* was stupid."

"Did you get drunk and jump out of a second floor window?"

"No, I dropped a bowling ball on it."

"That sounds more clumsy than stupid," said Paige.

"I did it on purpose."

"Why?"

"It was a bet."

"Did you win?"

"I sure did."

"How much?"

"Two dollars."

"You broke your foot on purpose for two dollars?"

"Remember when I said it was stupid?"

"I'd say you were right, but you're an adult and that would be inappropriate."

Jack laughed. "My older daughter would disagree with you, but I appreciate that. Anyway, if you guys don't mind, I'm going to look around to see if I can find any problem areas before the experts get here."

"Sounds good," said Adeline, mildly relieved that he didn't ask any more questions about Paige's fingers.

"I'll call you if we find anything that cracks the case, or if I've got any important updates on the banana."

- - -

The first movie didn't start for another hour, so they stopped at a park. Naomi ran straight for the swing set. Paige, far too old for such childish nonsense, sat on a bench with Adeline.

Adeline tapped Paige's bandaged hand. "Can we talk about this?"

"I guess."

"What happened?"

"I told you. I wasn't paying attention."

"You walk into a tree if you're not paying attention. You don't keep doing something that hurts."

"It didn't really hurt."

"Jamming things under somebody's fingernail is one of the best ways to torture information out of them. Of course it hurt."

Paige didn't respond.

"You don't have to talk about it if you don't want to," said Adeline. "We can save it for another time, if you're not comfortable."

"I was just a little foggy. I didn't feel very good."

"You felt sick?"

Paige shrugged. "A little."

"Why didn't you say that before?"

"It's not a good excuse. I should've clipped them later. They weren't that bad."

"Your dad felt sick, too. I hope they're able to find the problem today."

"Will we have to move if they don't?"

"I think so. We can't live in a house where everything is rotting, right?"

"I thought we had a lease."

"Legally, we can get out of it if we can prove that the house is unsafe. I think we can do that pretty easily." Adeline wasn't entirely sure that was true; she doubted there was precedent for tenants getting out of a lease because their food kept going bad. But they'd worry about that after today's house cleaning.

"Will Naomi and I still have our own rooms?"

"Yes. We wouldn't give you two your own rooms and then take it away. That would be child abuse."

"Mommy! Look at me!" shouted Naomi, who was swinging so high that it almost looked like she could do a loop-de-loop with a few more leg pumps.

"Not so high, sweetie!" Adeline called out. The last thing she needed was for Naomi to have a horrific swing set accident.

"I don't think you can go all the way around," said Paige.

"Well, we're not going to test that."

Naomi stopped actively swinging.

"For now we're going to pretend that everything is going to be completely fine," Adeline told Paige. "Jack was very nice about it, and I can't imagine there's a problem with the house that's so bad it can't be fixed."

"What if it was built on an ancient Indian burial ground?"

"You're not supposed to say 'Indian' unless you're talking about people from India."

"What if it was built on an ancient Indian burial ground where people from India were horribly murdered?"

"Then we should probably move."

- - -

Packing, moving, and unpacking had consumed so much of Adeline's recent life that it felt weird to relax in a movie theater seat. She felt guilty taking the day off when Boyd had to go to his stressful job, but he'd insisted and there wasn't much productive work she could do outside the house until the girls started school. So, the movies it was!

Neither film was particularly good. Adeline was not opposed to fart jokes, but they had to be *quality* fart jokes, and she did prefer that they be kept to fewer than thirty in a single motion picture. Naomi loved it. The second film in their double feature contained zero fart jokes and a surprising amount of courtroom intrigue for a kids' movie. Naomi did not enjoy this one quite as much.

When she drove back home late that afternoon, Jack's car and a green van were in the driveway. "Perfect timing!" said Jack as they walked through the front door. "They're just about done."

"Did they find anything wrong?" Adeline asked.

"Well, I've got good news and bad news. The bad news is, no, they didn't specifically find anything that could explain your problem. But they vacuumed all of the vents, changed the air filter even though it didn't really need it, gave the basement a thorough cleaning, and they even checked the attic. There really shouldn't be an issue."

"And the good news?"

"Follow me."

Adeline, Paige, and Naomi followed Jack into the kitchen. He gestured to the counter upon which the banana lay.

"Ta da!"

Adeline picked up the banana and inspected it. No brown spots. Plenty of green. She thought that *maybe* it was a bit more ripe than it should have been based on its condition this morning, but she also didn't typically apply that degree of scrutiny to a banana's life cycle. It definitely had not gone bad like the other fruit. Maybe they had indeed fixed the problem.

"Looks like a perfectly good banana," Adeline admitted. Now she kind of wondered if Jack thought they'd taken care of things, or if she'd been exaggerating. She supposed it didn't matter.

"And I've got a surprise for you," said Jack. "Come on out back."

He led them out to the backyard.

"Oh, cool!" shouted Naomi.

There were several fish in the koi pond. Naomi and Paige both crouched down to get a better look.

"An apology gift," said Jack.

"You really didn't have to do this," Adeline told him.

"No, but I don't like unsatisfied customers. Moving is enough of a pain in the butt without adding house problems into the mix."

"Well, we appreciate it. I'm sure Boyd would like to thank you in person."

"No need. Tell him I said hi. I'll get everybody cleared out of your home and we'll hope that everything is fine from here on out."

"I'm sure it will be. Thank you so much, Jack."

"Thanks for the fish!" said Naomi, who seemed transfixed.

"When I come back, I expect you to have names for all five of them."

"I will!"

A few minutes later, Jack and the cleaners were gone.

Adeline decided to keep monitoring the banana, just in case.

- - -

The banana was still in good shape when Boyd returned home from work.

"I think we may be okay," said Adeline, handing it to him. "This has been in the house all day."

"It's a miracle banana," Boyd declared.

"I've never been so excited about fruit. Maybe all it took was another go at the air ducts."

"Well, it's hard to describe just how much I did *not* want to pack everything up and start this process again. I would've put on a brave face, but on the inside I would've been bawling."

"I guess we don't know for sure that it's fixed. We'll keep watching the banana. Even if everything is fine now, we have to admit that it was weird, right?"

"Very weird."

- - -

It was difficult to justify "fruit no longer rotting" as a junk food celebration, so dinner was a healthy meal of salmon and Caesar salad.

- - -

Boyd lay on the couch, watching Netflix. There was still plenty to do around the house, but if the ladies got to spend their day at the movies, by God he was going to sit here and watch a young Bruce Willis take out some terrorists.

At least he was feeling better.

Mostly.

He'd felt fine at work and for a couple of hours after getting home, but now that he was plopped on the couch he was cold even with a blanket over him. Could just be the after effects. Getting rid of the root cause of his illness didn't mean that the illness would completely go away.

By the time he got to the part where Alan Rickman (*RIP to the best villain ever*) explained that they were not terrorists, but rather thieves, Boyd was back to feeling shitty.

- - -

Paige stared at herself in the mirror.

Even without the glasses that made her look like the world's biggest dork, she was ugly.

Everything about her was ugly.

Her nose was ugly. Her mouth was ugly. Her hands were ugly, and what kind of person had ugly hands? She didn't know anybody else who had to be embarrassed of their hands. Only her.

Her eyes. Those were the ugliest of them all.

She hadn't been lying to Mom and Dad or the doctor about not being able to feel the contact lens anymore, but she thought she could feel it now. It was way up there behind her eye. Would it even matter if she hurt herself trying to dig it out? Would she look any worse?

- - -

Adeline soaked in the hot bubble bath, thinking that this was absolute bliss. Candles. A glass of red wine. Soft music. If the kids were quiet, she was going to relax in here until she became the Hideous Prune Woman.

- - -

Billy.
Stardust.
Mrs. Swimmy.
Brinnaria.
Streaky.

Those were not necessarily the final names of the fish (Naomi had changed her mind over a dozen times) but that's what they were right now. Streaky, of course, was her favorite. He was white with a gold streak on his head.

They all looked hungry, but Naomi wasn't allowed to feed them without Mom or Dad being there. She could kill them if she gave them too much. She supposed this meant that the fish would eat and eat and eat until their stomachs exploded. Paige would probably want to see something like that, but not Naomi. She felt bad that the fish were so hungry, but she wasn't going to do anything that might hurt them.

She'd had goldfish before, but never big fish like this. These were so much better.

She couldn't stop watching them.

She wanted to crawl right in there and swim with them.

CHAPTER TWELVE
BEFORE

"Think it would kill the fish if we pissed in the koi pond?" asked Heck.

Maddox glared at him. "Fuck's the matter with you? We're here to make amends."

"It was a joke. And I'm not here to make amends to some King-Kong goldfish."

"Keep your voice down." The three of them had walked up to the front door, and then had a sudden realization that they should probably scope out the place first. They had no idea who lived here. Could be a house full of shotgun-toting, chainsaw-wielding hillbillies.

"We're wasting time," said Fletcher. "We need to just knock. What if she catches us sneaking around out here and then refuses to accept our apology?"

"How do you know it's a she?" asked Maddox.

Fletcher shrugged. "I just do. How do we know any of this?"

"I think he's right," said Heck. "I think it's a she."

"Yeah, I agree with that," said Maddox. He couldn't picture her in his mind, but, yeah, it was a she. That was much better than a house full of armed yokels.

The question of how they knew any of this was a very

good one. In fact, he'd rarely stopped thinking about it. But not understanding why they were compelled to confess their crimes and return the hard-earned cash that they desperately needed to somebody they didn't know...well, that just didn't feel like reason enough not to do it.

They walked back around the house to the front door.

"We should've worn nicer clothes," said Maddox, who'd worn a stained T-shirt to his sister's wedding.

He'd left the colostomy bag at home, of course, and also his gun. He hadn't even brought a knife. Hadn't even *considered* bringing a knife even though he was fairly certain that bringing a weapon was a good idea in this situation. He did have his share of the cash in a large yellow padded envelope. Heck and Fletcher had their own shares in similar envelopes. They could have put all of the cash in one, but Maddox had expressed concern that if, say, Heck returned the entire sum, he'd be the only one to get credit for it. Maddox couldn't take that risk. The other two men freely admitted that they'd been worried about the same thing, and so each of them returning their own third of the payment was unquestionably the right decision.

Maddox rang the doorbell.

They waited for a few moments.

"Ring it again," said Heck.

"What if she's just moving slow?" asked Maddox. "We don't want to make her mad."

"She's not going to fly into a rage because we rang the doorbell more than once."

"But it's late. The lights are out. We probably woke her up. She might not have even had a chance to get out of bed yet."

"Then that's a good reason to ring it again," said Maddox. "Let her know it's important."

He rang the doorbell again.

The porch light came on.

All three of the men took a step backwards.

The door swung open.

The woman appeared to be about fifty years old. You could make an argument that she wasn't bad looking, though she had kind of a spinster appearance, not that anybody used the word spinster anymore. Totally one of those crazy cat lady virgins.

She definitely wasn't frail, though. Not that she had muscles bulging through her nightgown, but Maddox got the sense that if she *was* ever married, she could've bashed her husband over the head with a shovel and buried him in the backyard without needing anybody's assistance.

She slowly raised her hand and pointed her index finger at Maddox. "Why hast thou disturbed my slumber?" she asked, in a low, eerie voice.

"I beg your pardon?"

"Relax, I'm kidding." She reached out and patted him on the shoulder. "Why's a big strong man like you such a scaredy-cat?"

"I wasn't scared," Maddox said.

"Of course you weren't."

"Saying 'I beg your pardon' isn't a sign of fear. I thought I misheard you."

"I think the gentleman doth protest too much. Would you like to come in? I don't typically have big strong men in my home, but since you're already here, it would be rude to turn you away."

"Yes, we'd love to," said Maddox. The woman stepped

aside as he, Heck, and Fletcher walked inside, making sure to wipe their feet on the doormat first.

The house was sparsely furnished. There weren't even any pictures on the walls.

"Nice place," said Heck, shutting the door behind him. Maddox felt like it could be a mistake to trap themselves inside, but it was too late now, and he didn't want to offend the woman by suggesting that she might pose a threat.

"Thank you," she said. "I don't need a home with three bedrooms, but I sometimes stay here between tenants. I like the area. And of course I was waiting for you. Which of you is Hector?"

Heck raised his hand.

"And Larry?"

"That's me," said Maddox.

The woman looked at Fletcher. "Then you must be Cliff."

Maddox had never known Fletcher's full name. He'd thought that Fletcher was his first name, not his last. He wanted to poke fun at him, but Cliff was a perfectly good name, unworthy of ridicule.

"Do you know my name?" she asked.

Maddox concentrated for a moment. "Virginia?"

"Close."

"Jean?"

"Closer."

"Gina?"

"That's it. Pleased to meet you. And you three have paid me this kind visit because you murdered my older sister, right?"

Maddox and his partners exchanged an uncertain glance. That was indeed the reason they were here, but it suddenly seemed unwise to just blurt it out.

"Yes," Maddox admitted. "It wasn't our idea."

"That makes it all better then?"

"No, of course not. But we only did it for the money. We didn't know she was your sister. Or even anybody's sister."

"You knew she was at least somebody's daughter."

"Well, yes, that's true, but, I mean, we didn't know if her parents were still alive." Maddox didn't feel that he was doing himself any favors. Why the hell did he have to do all of the heavy lifting in this conversation? Why weren't Heck and Fletcher trying to help him out?

"Only for the money," said Gina. "Was it worth it?"

"No. Not at all. Not one bit."

Maddox looked over at Heck for assistance.

"Not at all," Heck agreed.

Maddox held up his envelope. "We brought the money. Every dollar. We wanted to give it to you, as penance."

"I see." Gina kind of smiled at him. That is, her mouth didn't curl up, but she seemed to be smiling with her eyes. "Have you noticed anything unusual since you've been here?"

"No, ma'am."

"Do I seem like an impolite host?"

"No."

"I invited you into my home, and yet here we are, standing around. I didn't offer you a seat on my comfortable sofa. I haven't asked if I could get you something to drink. Do you know why this is? Let Cliff answer; he hasn't spoken much."

"I don't know," said Fletcher.

"It's because I do not like you. You are unintelligent

men who are easily manipulated. It creates a dilemma for me, because I need you to be easily manipulated to work my witchcraft, but it disgusts me that I'm successful. You do understand that you're not here of your own free will, right?"

The three men nodded.

"Good. I'm glad you're not that stupid. You let yourselves be paid to do something very, very naughty. Naughtier than you even know. Something that an extremely bad person hoped to use to gain some power that didn't belong to him. Sadly for him, it didn't work. And sadly for you, I'm quite unhappy about it."

"We brought the money, though," said Maddox. "It's yours. All three of us agreed."

"Let's take this to the kitchen, shall we?" Without waiting for an answer, Gina walked down the hallway.

Maddox believed that this was an excellent opportunity for them to flee the house, and maybe the country. And yet he couldn't bring himself to do it. The thing Gina had said about him being easily manipulated was clearly true, and apparently there was nothing he could do about it.

They followed her.

"Throw the money in the sink, please," she said.

Maddox, Heck, and Fletcher tossed their envelopes into the sink.

"You can count it if you want," said Maddox.

"I trust you. Do any of you smoke?"

"Heck does," said Maddox, accusingly. He assumed that Gina did not approve of smokers.

"Does that mean you have a lighter in your pocket?" Gina asked him.

"Yeah."

"Well, don't stand there like an imbecile. I wouldn't ask you if you had a lighter in your pocket if I didn't mean for you to take it out."

"Sorry, sorry." Heck dug into his pocket and pulled out a black lighter. A few coins and a pack of gum fell to the floor along with it, but he didn't pick them up. He extended the lighter toward Gina.

"No, it's more fun if you do it," she said. "Burn the money."

"What?" Maddox asked.

"Burn the blood money."

"Don't you want it?"

"I'm not saying I couldn't use it. I'd love the extra cash. But, no, I do not want the money you were paid to murder my sister. I wouldn't even accept it to donate to charity. I want it destroyed. If you thought this was how you were going to cleanse your conscience, I'm afraid you were wrong."

She picked up a container of lighter fluid. Since people rarely kept tins of lighter fluid next to their kitchen sink, Maddox was pretty sure she'd planned all of this out before they arrived.

"Can we just keep the money?" Heck asked.

The sheer stupidity of his question should have made everybody chuckle, but Maddox was terrified that Gina would be outraged instead of amused.

She narrowed her eyes. Though she definitely wasn't amused, she didn't seem to be filled with rage, so that was a relief. "No," she said. "You may not keep the money."

"I understand," said Heck. "I shouldn't have asked."

Gina squirted a generous amount of lighter fluid onto the envelopes. "Light them up," she said. "Be careful that you don't burn yourself. I've got an ice pack in the freezer and bandages in the bathroom, but I will not offer them to you. If your skin gets red and blistered, you're on your own. Burn the money."

Heck flicked on the flame. "It's a lot of money," he said.

"Yes, it most certainly is. If only you'd earned it honestly. Burn the money, Hector. Please do not make me ask you again."

Heck dropped the lighter into the sink. The flames whooshed up into the air, almost getting his hand. Maddox could see the bills as the yellow envelope burned away and felt heartsick. That cash was supposed to solve a lot of his problems.

Everybody stood there, silently watching the money turn to ashes.

After it was gone far beyond the point of salvage, Gina turned on the faucet and doused the remaining flames. "Don't you all feel better, knowing that this filthy, dirty, wretched money is gone?"

Maddox didn't, but he lied and said, "Yes."

"Good. I know I do."

"Anyway, that's why we came here. Penance."

"Right, right. You'd said that earlier. Are you up for a hypothetical discussion, Larry?"

"Of course."

"Let's pretend that you stole an apple. A nice, juicy, red apple. But let's say that the owner of the apple caught you before you ate it. So you gave it back. Would you consider that doing penance?"

Maddox said nothing.

"Or let's say that you did eat the apple. After the owner caught you, you went straight to the market and bought them another apple. A better, juicier, redder apple. Does *that* count as penance?"

"I think it makes things right."

"Perhaps," said Gina. "But we weren't talking about balancing out the universe. We were talking about doing penance. Maybe you just used the wrong word; after all, we've already established that you're not very smart. But the word 'penance' is out there and there's no taking it back now. What I'm trying to say through this hypothetical example is that burning the money you received for taking my sister away from me isn't good enough."

"What do you want?"

"What can you offer?"

Maddox shrugged. "I'm not sure."

"I've got a question for all three of you. Anybody can answer. Did you truly believe when you walked into my home that you were going to live to see sunrise?"

Nobody answered.

"Go on, don't be shy," Gina urged. "I want to know the answer. Did you honestly think that you were not going to die tonight? Were you somehow under the impression that I would spare you a grisly, excruciating, horrific death?"

"I—" said Maddox.

"I'm kidding again," said Gina. "I know that I'm pulling most of the strings right now and you're not making decisions that are in your best interest. But to end the suspense, yes, all three of you are going to die."

The three of them could, of course, overpower this woman—Maddox's mind refused to let him think of her as a "bitch," even though it was a word he used on a regular basis—pretty easily. But Maddox had no intention of resisting her, and he knew Heck and Fletcher wouldn't either.

He was frightened of death, yet felt no compulsion to beg for his life.

If she wanted to kill him, then, yeah, that's what was going to happen.

"I think I've been too nice to you, all things considered," said Gina. "I've been keeping your emotions in check. It seems unfair to you boys not to let you fully experience the all-night horror show of what's about to happen."

The sheer terror of the situation hit Maddox all at once. Tears flowed. He dropped to his knees without shame and held his fists together, almost like a cartoonish parody of somebody pleading for his life.

"Don't do it," he said, sobbing. "Please, please, please, God, don't kill us."

Heck and Fletcher dropped to their knees as well.

"Knock it off, you pathetic pieces of shit," said Gina. "Lucky for you I'm not as depraved as you are, so it won't be as bad for you as it was for my sister. Don't get me wrong; it's still going to be terrible."

"We'll do anything," said Fletcher.

"You're goddamn right you will. Who wants to be first?"

CHAPTER THIRTEEN

Adeline closed her eyes, thinking she could almost drift off to sleep.

She suddenly awoke with a start. She hadn't even realized she'd fallen asleep—it felt like she just closed her eyes for a couple of seconds—but the water was lukewarm.

The suds didn't look any different.

She held up her hand. Her fingers weren't wrinkled.

In fact, the water seemed to be getting colder.

Much colder.

As she watched in shock, some ice crystals formed on the surface.

Small chunks of ice floated to the top.

Clearly, she *had* fallen asleep and not actually woken up yet. Unless she was suddenly in the void of outer space, there was no environment in which a hot bath would start to immediately freeze up like this.

And then she knew she wasn't dreaming because the water was so cold that it stung.

She grabbed the sides of the tub and pushed herself up, shards of ice sticking to her belly. Her legs were so cold that she couldn't bend her knees to stand up. The water turned to ice all around her as she cried out for help.

- - -

Paige flinched as she heard her mother shout for Dad to help her.

She didn't sound like she was trying to be funny. In fact, she sounded genuinely scared.

Paige should go see what was wrong.

But was there anything she could do? What if she made things worse? What if by rushing out of her bedroom she actually messed everything up?

She didn't want to distract herself from the job of fixing her face. This was important work and it required intense concentration.

Mom or face? Mom or face?

Mom was more important. She'd do what she could to help.

Paige lowered the scissors from her eye.

- - -

Boyd tossed the blanket aside, sat up, and got up off the couch. Then he lost his balance and tumbled onto the hardwood floor. He landed hard on his right arm, but didn't seem to have actually injured it, although he was suddenly so dizzy that it was difficult to tell for sure.

He felt sick to his stomach.

His forehead was drenched with sweat.

He tried to get up but the room felt like it was spinning. But if Adeline was crying out for help, he couldn't wait for the dizzy spell to wear off. He had to get right up, even if it meant smashing into the wall.

His arms and legs weren't working properly. His body felt like he was burning up from the inside, as if he'd been instantly stricken with a dangerously high fever. The worst flu symptoms he'd ever experienced, combined, all at once.

Was he dying?

He tried to shout to Adeline, but his mouth had gone completely dry and he couldn't make any noise beyond a feeble grunt. Forget the dizziness; his vision was so blurred that he didn't even know which direction he was facing.

Maybe he really was going to die.

He didn't feel like he was going to lose consciousness, though. He'd have to fight through this. Get Paige's attention so she'd call 911.

Paige would've heard Adeline, right? Naomi was outside, but Paige was in her bedroom, and even with the door closed she would've heard her mother cry out. Paige would save the day. An ambulance would be here soon.

- - -

Adeline hit the bathroom floor, ice stuck all over the lower half of her body. Some of the ice shattered on impact, and some dug into her red skin. The pain was excruciating. She grabbed the bottom corner of a towel and yanked it off the hook so that her daughters wouldn't see her sprawled naked on the floor.

Her legs were bleeding in a few places where the ice had jabbed into her skin after she struck the tile. She threw the towel over herself and called out for Boyd again. Why hadn't he answered?

"Paige! Come in here, honey! I need you!"

Adeline forced herself not to sob. She was terrified but she had to be brave until they figured out what was going on.

What *could* be happening? Hot water in a bathtub did not freeze like this.

They were getting out of this nightmare of a house. Today. And never coming back. She didn't care if they had to pay people to come get their stuff and rack up credit card debt while they stayed in a hotel, the Gardner family was done with this hellhole.

What if there was permanent damage to her legs? What if they were frostbitten?

God, she was in agony. Where the hell were Boyd and Paige?

- - -

"Paige! Come in here, honey! I need you!"

Paige opened the door but stopped right before leaving her room. Yes, Mom needed help. Why hadn't Dad responded to her cries? Paige needed to find out exactly what was happening and do whatever she could to assist both of them.

But what if they were repulsed by her?

What if she walked out there, and Mom and Dad were so sickened by her hideous appearance that they sent her away? They'd never sent her away before this, but that didn't mean they wouldn't suddenly realize what a monster they had for a daughter.

She couldn't do it. She couldn't leave her room.

Paige turned back toward her mirror. She wanted to

smash her fists into it, shatter it. If she did that, though, she wouldn't be able to see when she carefully removed the contact lens from the top of her eye with the scissors. She deserved to have a sharp piece of metal jammed deep into her eye socket, but didn't want to do it herself.

She was just going to cut away the lid. Get it out of the way so she could reach the contact lens. She honestly wasn't sure why the doctor hadn't thought to do that. Maybe he was so distracted by her ghastly appearance that he forgot how to do his job.

She winced. It felt like the lens was tightening around her eyeball.

Constricting like a snake.

What if it crushed her eye, sending a spurt of jelly flying across the room onto the mirror?

She had to get it out.

Breathing deeply, bracing herself for what needed to be done, Paige kicked her bedroom door shut.

- - -

Boyd didn't know for certain that he was dragging himself toward the sound of Adeline's voice. He thought he was. But not only had his vision gone from blurry to almost completely black, there was now a ringing in his ears so loud that Adeline sounded like she was calling out from miles away.

His head struck the wall. He couldn't tell, through pain or the sound, how hard he'd hit it.

He tried once again to let Adeline know that he was on his way, even though that was essentially a lie. It didn't matter; he couldn't speak anyway.

It was hard to breathe.

He was almost positive he was going to die, and he wasn't ready. His daughters were too young. Adeline needed his help. He couldn't die here, lying on the floor, plagued by some sickness he couldn't even explain.

He gritted his teeth—thinking he may have bit down on his tongue; he could taste the blood but not feel the pain—and tried to crawl some more. It felt like wasted effort, since what was he going to do for anybody while in this condition? But he certainly couldn't just wait around to die.

His head was pounding so violently that he literally believed that something might be trying to escape from it. Literally. At this point, why couldn't there be a creature inside there, hammering with its clawed fists, cracking his skull a bit more with each punch? Soon it would shatter his cranium, wriggle its way out, and slither away to wreak havoc.

Would it *really* be so bad if he died now?

Yes. He wasn't ready to die.

But he wasn't sure he had a choice.

- - -

Adeline grabbed the sink and pulled herself to a standing position. Her legs didn't want to cooperate, but she managed to stay upright. She let go of the sink for a couple of seconds, to test whether or not she'd immediately lose her balance and drop right back down to the tile. She didn't.

"Seriously, Boyd! Where are you? Is everything okay?"

The towel fell to the floor. She wasn't going to keep messing with it.

Was her cell phone in her bedroom, or in the living

room? She couldn't remember if she'd just set it down, or plugged it in to charge.

Bedroom. She was pretty sure.

She took a step. Her knee wobbled but she didn't fall.

She did two more steps on her own. Some pieces of ice slid away, and the pain was already starting to subside. She was sure she'd be okay. And, with the panic fading, she assumed that Boyd and Paige had simply gone outside to join Naomi by the koi pond. Which didn't mean they weren't still getting the hell out of this house as soon as possible...

From where she stood now, she was close enough to brace herself against the doorway. She stepped into the hallway. At the other end, in the living room, Boyd lay on the floor, drenched in perspiration, skin pale, eyes wide open.

"Boyd!"

He looked up, but in the wrong direction.

Then he vomited. Adeline couldn't tell how much of it was chicken Caesar salad, but a lot of it was blood.

- - -

Mommy and Daddy had warned Naomi not to wade into the pond or even lean too close to it. It was a dumb warning, because the pond was so shallow that even a baby couldn't drown itself in there, but Naomi had promised them that she'd behave.

Now she wasn't so sure she wanted to keep her promise.

They'd know she'd been in the pond because her clothes would get wet. But if she hurried back inside when she was done and changed them before they saw her, she could get away with it. She'd be careful not to leave wet footprints on the floor.

She stuck her index finger into the water.

Very cold. Splashing around in there might not be as fun as she thought.

Some bubbles came up from the bottom. That was weird. What was making that happen?

More and more bubbles appeared, like the water was starting to boil, even though it was still cold. Naomi pulled her finger out, just in case.

Stardust, her favorite, rolled onto his back and floated on the surface.

Naomi gasped. Was he dead?

Then Billy did the same thing. Naomi knew perfectly well that fish were dead when they floated like that, but she didn't want to believe it. Was it her fault? Had she poisoned the water when she stuck her finger in it? Was that why Mommy and Daddy had told her to stay away from it?

Her other three fish went belly-up, all at the same time.

This had to be her fault.

The water was still bubbling. Not at a full boil like when somebody was making macaroni and cheese, but a constant stream of tiny bubbles.

Stardust's skin was coming off.

All five fish were breaking apart. Scales floated next to them. Blood and guts poured out of their bodies and mixed into the water.

Naomi stood there, frozen with horror.

It wasn't long before nothing remained of her new pets except fish heads and tails connected by bones. The koi pond, which had been her favorite part of the new house minutes ago, was just filled with fish soup.

It smelled *awful*.

Rotten.

And something else was moving in the water.

\- - -

Boyd wiped his mouth off on his sleeve. Vomiting blood was a sign that something was seriously wrong...yet he suddenly felt immensely better, like when a fever breaks. His vision was clear. His head had stopped pounding. He could think again.

A scream.

He and Adeline both turned toward Paige's closed door.

The door opened and Paige stumbled into the hallway, a pair of scissors in one hand, the other hand pressed tightly over her eye.

"*I don't know what I did!*" she wailed. "*I don't know what I did!*"

Boyd got up and rushed over to her. Adeline, who must've leapt out of her bubble bath without even taking the time to wrap a towel around her, limped over to them as well.

"Let me see," said Boyd.

"I think I hurt myself!"

"Move your hand, Paige."

"Honey, move your hand," said Adeline.

"Throw on some clothes," Boyd told her. "I've got this. Paige, honey, move your hand so we can see what's wrong."

Paige began to sob. "I wasn't thinking right! I would never do this to myself! Everything in my head was messed up!"

Boyd wrapped his fingers around her hand and pulled it away from her face.

He let out an involuntary gasp at the blood.

"Oh, shit."

"Did I cut my eye?"

She'd cut the side of her eyelid for sure. (With a pair of scissors? Had she actually slid the blade under her eyelid?) But it wasn't hanging down in a flap. It might not be as bad as it looked. She was thrashing around too much for him to be able to tell if she'd cut her actual eye or not.

"Keep your head still," Boyd told her.

"I don't know why I did it."

"It's okay, honey. I lost control of myself, too. There's something wrong and it's not your fault."

Adeline came out of the bathroom in sweatpants, still putting on the T-shirt she'd been wearing before her bath. "How is she?"

"It might not be that bad," said Boyd. Adeline's gasp, much louder than his had been, did not help sell that idea to their daughter. The amount of blood was unnerving, but it didn't mean there was any permanent damage. "I don't want to touch it and hurt her more."

"Let's go to the emergency room. For both of you."

Boyd nodded. "Why were you calling us?"

"I'll get Paige to the car. You take a quick look in the bathroom."

Boyd couldn't imagine what could be in the bathroom that would take priority—even if it was only for a two-second peek—over getting Paige to the hospital. He quickly walked down the hallway, amazed at how quickly he'd recovered from an illness where he'd thought he was moments from death, and looked into the bathroom.

There were several chunks of ice on the floor. He went inside for a closer look. The water in the bathtub had frozen solid.

That was...not normal.

From outside, Naomi shrieked.

- - -

A hand came out of the cloudy water, even though the koi pond wasn't anywhere near deep enough for somebody to be hidden in there. The only way this could really be happening was if Naomi was seeing an arm that wasn't attached to a body.

It kind of looked like maybe the hand was made out of water. She could see through it, sort of.

Then a man climbed out of the pond. A full-sized man. He was a lot taller and bigger than Dad, and his head was completely bald.

Naomi didn't think he was made out of water. She thought he was a ghost. She'd been told that ghosts weren't real enough times to finally believe it, but she also had to trust what she could see right in front of her.

The man stood on the edge of the pond. No water was dripping off of him. He looked around, like somebody who couldn't figure out how he'd gotten there. Then he looked at Naomi.

He opened his mouth as if he wanted to say something to her.

Then he made gasping sounds, like he was choking to death. He put his hands over his neck and doubled over.

Naomi realized that this was the time to scream and run.

CHAPTER FOURTEEN
BEFORE

"**H**im!" shouted Maddox, pointing at Fletcher. "Kill him first!"

Heck frantically nodded. "Yes! Yes! He deserves it more!"

Fletcher opened his mouth as if he wanted to defend himself, then silently wept instead. The sight of a great big guy on his knees, tears streaming down his face, shoulders quivering, was one of the most pathetic things Maddox had ever seen. He hoped that Gina agreed so she'd kill Fletcher first.

"Shut up, both of you," said Gina. "I was asking for volunteers, not suggestions."

"I swear, we won't tell—" Maddox began.

"Stop it. Stop right there. You're welcome to beg and blubber and wet yourselves and do whatever it takes to express your fear. But don't insult my intelligence by lying and saying that you'd just leave here and never speak of it again. You're the dumb ones, not me. Remember that. Apologize."

"I'm sorry," said Maddox.

"That said, yes, I believe that Mr. Cliff Fletcher will be the first casualty of the night."

Fletcher slumped over, his bald head almost touching the floor.

"Thank you," said Maddox, so delirious with relief that he didn't even care how ridiculous it was to thank her. "Thank you so much."

"I think we'll head outside," said Gina. "My neighbors aren't up in my business, but they're close enough to hear you guys bellowing outside, so I'm going to ask you to keep the volume down. You can handle that, right?"

"We can," said Heck. "We can, I promise. We won't make a peep."

"Get up, all of you," said Gina. "I know you're afraid but try to have some respect for yourselves."

Maddox, Heck, and Fletcher stood up, quickly.

"Let's go. It's already late, and you're going to be suffering for quite some time, so we need to get this train moving."

They followed her down the hallway. She opened the front door and they followed her outside and around to the back of the house, by the koi pond.

"Step into the pond," Gina told Fletcher. "Don't worry, the fish won't bite you."

"Do I have to?" Fletcher asked in a soft, scared voice.

"What do you think?"

Fletcher waded into the center of the pond. At its deepest, it didn't even come up to his knees. Maddox felt bad for the poor bastard, but it was right that he should die first. Tough shit for him.

"This would be easier if we could do it in the deep end of a swimming pool, but we can work with this. What you're going to do for me, Cliff, is drown yourself."

Fletcher shook his head.

"Are you saying no to me?"

"Please, Gina. There has to be another way."

"There is. Two other ways, actually. And by that I'm referring to the much worse ways that your friends are going to die. You won't be alive to consider yourself fortunate, but trust me, you're getting off easy."

"Okay."

"Not that drowning is the kind of death somebody should aspire to. When that cold water starts going into your lungs you won't feel very lucky, believe me. It's an awful, awful way to go. Take a deep breath before you dunk your head under the water. That'll give you just a bit longer to live. Now, when you can't hold your breath any longer, the panic will set in. Few things cause more sheer panic than drowning, and you're going to want to lift your head out of the water, but know that if you do, I will be so enraged that your death will make the fates of your friends seem like they died in their sleep after a night of great sex. Do not lift your head out of the water. I don't care how scared you get, how much your lungs burn, how much it feels like your chest is going to explode, keep your head under the water. Do you understand me?"

"I understand," said Fletcher, sounding like a scolded five-year-old.

"Do you have any final words? If so, keep them to yourself. I don't wish to hear them. Drown yourself."

Fletcher knelt down into the pond and dunked his head under the water.

"That's right, you murderous piece of garbage. Gasp for breath under there. Take in that water." Instead of speaking loudly, as if trying to be heard underwater, Gina was whispering. These words were clearly for her own benefit. "Agony. I want you to die in absolute agony."

Her voice softened even more, to the point where Maddox couldn't quite hear what she was saying, but her eye was twitching in anger and this was clearly less about wicked mockery than simple fury.

Fletcher's body began to thrash.

"Stay under there," said Gina.

The thrashing became more and more violent.

Maddox didn't think he could drown himself. It didn't matter if a worse punishment awaited him above the water; if you couldn't breathe, you were going to seek air, no matter what.

"That's right, suffer!" said Gina, no longer speaking as quietly. "Suffer, you son of a bitch. I hope it hurts. I hope it fucking hurts." She wiped away a tear.

After several hard-to-watch moments, Fletcher finally stopped moving. His body floated to the surface, facedown.

"My neighbors mind their own business, but I still shouldn't leave a dead body floating in my koi pond," said Gina. "Besides, I don't know if the fish will start eating him. No reason to make this more grisly than it needs to be. Could you pull him out of there? Just drag him off to the side. I'll take care of the body after you two are dead."

Both Maddox and Heck splashed into the pool, each of them taking one of Fletcher's arms. As they dragged the corpse out of the pond, Maddox hoped Gina noticed that he was doing more of the work, and would reward him by killing Heck first.

"That's fine," said Gina as they pulled the corpse onto the grass. "I didn't want to see him all bloated with bites taken out of him. Let's go back inside."

Maddox and Heck followed her into the house. Gina

asked if she could get either of them something to drink, but Maddox knew she was just teasing.

"Basement time!" said Gina. "That's where your true penance begins."

They walked down the stairs into the basement. Maddox didn't like seeing the large plastic tarp spread out on the cement floor. He also didn't like seeing the axe. He wanted to say something funny to lighten the mood, maybe something about being surprised that she cut firewood in her basement, but he couldn't get the words to connect in his brain.

"I have to warn you, things are about to become very gruesome," said Gina. "Hector is about to regret some of his recent life choices."

"It wasn't me," Heck insisted. He pointed to Maddox. "He set everything up! This would never have happened if it wasn't for him!"

"That's why you're the one to be dismembered," Gina explained. "You'll bleed out pretty quickly once your arms and legs start coming off. At least I assume you will. I've never done this before."

"I can't," said Heck. "I can't do it."

"Did you think I meant for you to chop *yourself* up?" Gina giggled. "A hand or a foot, maybe, but I don't see how it would work beyond that. I'd never ask you to do something so depraved."

She walked over and picked up the axe.

"Lie on the floor," she said. "Spread-eagle."

"I don't know what that means."

"Spread-eagle?"

"Right."

"Really? I thought everybody knew that term. I'm pretty sure it's not a regional thing. It means to put your arms and legs out, sort of like you're making a snow angel, but don't move them."

Heck lay facedown on the tarp and extended his arms and legs.

"Oh, no, no, no. You have to see what's coming. Roll over."

Heck rolled over. Maddox wasn't sure if his intention had been to hide from the sight of the axe blade falling upon him, or if he didn't want anybody to see him cry. Maddox, personally, didn't care who saw him cry anymore.

Gina turned to Maddox. "Be a dear and grab the roll of duct tape that's on the shelf over there, will you? Even if he tries his best to be brave, I'm sure your friend will be noisy."

Maddox went over and got the roll of tape. He extended it to her.

"A gentleman would offer to do it for me."

"Sorry." Maddox knelt down beside Heck and duct taped his mouth shut.

"Thank you. Keep the roll handy; we'll need it again in a bit. Step off the tarp, please."

Maddox walked off the tarp. He didn't want to see what was about to happen, but he knew that Gina would make him watch, so there was no reason to even pretend that he could look away.

Gina stepped over to Heck. "We both know this is going to hurt. I won't pretend otherwise. Still, count your blessings. You're the psychopath, not me. I could chop off your fingers, one at a time, and then your toes, and then your ears, and then your disgusting, disease-ridden penis. But I'm not up for that level of torment." She raised the axe over her head. "We'll keep this simple."

She slammed the axe down on his right arm, just below the shoulder. Heck screamed, muffled by the duct tape. Though Maddox had seen worse than this during the massacre of Gina's sister, he still gasped and put his hand over his mouth. Gina twisted the axe to pop his arm off all the way.

"Nobody said you could close your eyes," Gina told Heck. "Open them. Watch yourself bleed. Watch every goddamn drop spew out of your body."

Heck opened his eyes.

"That's right, you evil piece of shit. No blindfold. No going to your happy place."

She slammed the axe down upon his other arm. This time she got him just above the elbow. Maddox had done a good job with the duct tape. It stayed on and the neighbors wouldn't hear anything. He hoped that Gina noticed and appreciated how well he'd done.

"I could do some sick things with your severed arms," Gina said. "Repulsive, mentally ill things. I'm not going to. Keep those words in your head: *This could be worse.*"

Heck didn't look like he agreed.

"Your legs are next," Gina informed him. "I'll do my best, but I can't promise to lop them off in one swing. Maybe your buddy here could, but I wouldn't ask him to do anything that might mess with your friendship."

She hoisted the axe over her head, then brought it down upon his upper left thigh. It sunk deep but not nearly enough to sever the limb. Gina pried the blade out of his leg.

"I'll try to hit it in the same place," she said, raising the axe again.

She slammed the axe down upon the leg. She did not hit him in the same place.

It took several more swings to remove the leg. Gina wiped some blood from her face and glanced over at Maddox. "This is more of a workout than I expected. I don't know how lumberjacks do it all day."

Heck's eyes were still open, wide with terror.

"I'll try to do better when I chop off the other leg," said Gina, breathing heavily. "My arms are getting sore, though, so I might do worse."

She did indeed do worse, but as far as Maddox could tell, Heck bled to death before she was finished and he didn't have to feel the last six or seven swings.

"I said I wasn't going to mutilate him for no reason, but the job seems unfinished if he still has his head," said Gina. She swung the axe at his neck, decapitating him in a single swing. Then she tossed the axe to the floor.

Gina's shoes made wet squishy sounds as she walked to the edge of the tarp toward Maddox. Blood dripped from her clothes.

"I need to take a break," she said. "I'm not as young as I used to be."

"That's fine," said Maddox.

She stood there for a couple of minutes, catching her breath. Maddox was going to die. He was going to die horribly. There was nothing he could do to stop it.

"Do you have kids?" Gina asked.

"A son."

"Does he live with you?"

"No."

"Ever see him?"

"Not really."

"So not having a father anymore isn't really going to impact his life, huh?"

"I guess not."

"Are you scared, Larry?"

"Yeah."

"How scared?"

"After what you did to Fletcher and Heck? How scared do you think?"

Oh, crap, he hoped he wasn't being rude.

"I wish I could turn off what I was doing to your mind," said Gina. "It's making you less afraid. However scared you're feeling right now, it's not even a fraction of the terror you'd be experiencing if I wasn't doing some puppeteering. I'd love to know that you were getting the full impact of what's happening to you...but, of course, you'd become dangerous to me. I can't have you fighting back and escaping, now can I?"

"I wouldn't fight back," said Maddox.

"Now, now, we both know that isn't true. My arms are feeling better, so I think it's time to get back to work. I don't feel like cleaning up two separate messes, which means that I'm going to need you to lie down next to your friend."

Maddox walked over to Heck's dismembered corpse. He slid Heck's right arm and leg out of the way with his foot, then lay down in the pool of blood next to his torso. It immediately soaked the back of his clothes. At least it was warm and didn't get in his ears.

"I hope it's not too wet and sticky," said Gina. "Do you know what I like, Larry?"

"What?"

"I like bones. That's not innuendo. I mean literal bones. I've always been fascinated by them. I think they're beautiful, don't you?"

"Yes."

"You don't have to agree with me. I know it's a quirk."

Gina walked over to one of the shelves. "I want to see your bones, Larry. Right now, my plan is to expose all two hundred and six of them. I might be less ambitious by the time I quit."

"You're going to cut me open?"

Gina shook her head. "Nothing so precise. This isn't surgery." She picked up a fireplace poker. "I don't have a fireplace, but I knew you were coming so I bought this special. Still has the sticker on it."

"Do you really have to do this?" Maddox asked.

"I'm trying not to show it, but I'm very, very pissed off. When you ask stupid questions, you piss me off even more. Yes, my plan is to beat you with this poker until your bones break through your flesh, so I guess from your perspective it doesn't matter if I'm angry or not, but still, if you're going to die, why end on a note of stupidity?"

"I didn't think it was a stupid question. There has to be a way we can work this out. I can be your personal servant."

"What an offer. I can spend every waking moment around somebody I despise. Sorry, not interested." Gina sighed. "However, now that I've criticized your stupidity, I just realized that I skipped a step. I can't see your bones burst through your skin if you're wearing clothes. So I'm going to need you to get up and strip."

Maddox sat up. Blood ran down his back.

"This isn't about perversion, so keep your underwear on, but everything else goes."

Maddox slowly untied his shoes, pulled them off, and tossed them off the tarp. Then he removed his socks and tossed them aside as well.

"Do it faster," said Gina. "We're not in any hurry, but

when you undress that slowly it feels like seduction."

Maddox stood up and took off the rest of his clothes except his blood-soaked briefs.

"Perfect. Now lie back down."

Maddox lay back down in the blood. He could feel a small piece of meat under his shoulder blade and wondered if Gina would be upset if he sat up and pushed it away. He decided not to risk it.

She tapped the end of the poker against his shin. "I think this would be one of the most painful bones to shatter. Do you agree?"

"Yes."

"Forgot the tape. I can't seem to get it together, can I?" She wasn't taunting him. Gina seemed genuinely annoyed at the skipped steps. She went over and got the duct tape, then brought it to Maddox. "You know what to do."

Maddox sat up and wrapped the tape around his mouth, winding it three times around his head to make sure it didn't come loose. He gave her back the tape then lay down in the wetness again.

"Thank you," said Gina. She placed the roll of tape on a shelf and then returned to the tarp. "Okay, I think we're ready to see how many of your bones I can expose."

Maddox braced himself for the pain. She brought the fireplace poker down hard upon his left shin. The pain was far more intense than Maddox was expecting, and he screamed. A bone broke for certain, but no sharp end protruded from his leg.

"I didn't expect it to work on the first try," said Gina.

It worked on the fourth try.

In theory, Maddox should have eventually become

numb to the pain, but apparently it took more than two broken legs and two broken arms to reach that point. Every blow of the poker hurt just as much as the one before it.

He lay there, weeping, appendages twisted and mangled. Gina rested the poker against the wall. "I need a break," she said. "I'm going upstairs to lie on my couch for ten, fifteen minutes with a glass of White Zinfandel. Don't go anywhere."

Gina went upstairs, shutting off the light behind her.

Maddox lay in the dark, wishing he could die. He was afraid of death in a big way, but he needed this misery to end. It wasn't fair that Heck and Fletcher got off so easy. He wasn't any worse than them. He didn't deserve this.

Maybe he'd be rescued.

A while later, the light turned back on. It was Gina who came downstairs, not a guardian angel, and she looked well rested. She smiled at him as she picked up the poker.

"You didn't escape. Did you even try?"

Maddox shook his head.

"I don't blame you. I wouldn't want to jiggle around those shattered bones either. Ouch. So it really doesn't look like you're much of a flight risk. Do you know what that means?"

Maddox shook his head again.

"It means that I can release my mental grip on you. Give you the full experience. The level of pain will be the same, but if you think you're scared now..."

She didn't snap her fingers or anything like that. Maddox's awareness returned to him, all at once. The realization that he'd been suicidally stupid in showing up at Gina's house to return the money. The horror of watching his friends—and, yes, he considered Heck and Fletcher his closest friends—die ghastly deaths. And the complete understanding that he was close to death himself.

He screamed and screamed and screamed.

Gina laughed.

"I'm not ready for this to end, so I'm going to keep working on your arms and legs. Then I'll move on to your ribs. I really hope you're still alive to get to see a few of your broken ribs. Eventually one of your bones will puncture a lung or something and you'll die. And I bet you think that's the end, don't you?"

Maddox didn't respond.

"Your friend's suffering didn't end when his body stopped twitching in the water. And just because your other friend's severed head is right next to you doesn't mean he's at peace. Oh, no. They're not having a good time right now. Not at all."

Maddox wished he could speak through the duct tape. He would have asked, "Are they in Hell?"

Gina smashed the poker against his left wrist.

She smiled as if she'd heard his unspoken question.

"Close enough," she said.

Before dawn, Maddox joined them.

CHAPTER FIFTEEN

Naomi ran to the back door. She grabbed the doorknob, but she was so scared and her hands were so sweaty that she couldn't get it to turn. The door was covered with large brown spots that hadn't been there before.

She looked over her shoulder. The man had stood back up and was coming after her. Though he wasn't far, he was stumbling around, and still clutched his neck.

He dropped to his knees.

Did he need help?

Naomi got the doorknob to turn. As she threw open the door, she noticed that a couple of the brown spots were getting larger, like soda coming out of a can somebody had dropped on the floor.

She took one last look at the man, who was reaching for her even though he was much too far away to actually grab her, then rushed into the house and pulled the door closed behind her. The brown spots were on the inside of the door, too, along with some greenish ones.

Mommy and Daddy were in the hallway. Now that she was safe, Naomi had no need to try to be brave. She stood there and screamed.

- - -

Adeline crouched down and put her arms around Naomi. "It's okay, honey. It's okay. What happened?"

Naomi continued screaming.

"What's wrong with her?" asked Paige, sounding on the verge of panic. A tiny amount of blood had already soaked through the washcloth she'd pressed against her eye.

Boyd walked over to the door. What the hell was happening to the wood? It looked like it was rotting right in front of his eyes.

Naomi stopped screaming and began sobbing instead. "There's—there's—there's—"

There was a loud *thud* on the other side of the door and it shook on its hinges. Boyd took a great big step back.

"Naomi?" he asked. "Who's out there?"

The door shook again.

Boyd went over to peek through one of the windows. He pulled back the curtain. The glass was filled with tiny bubbles, so many that he couldn't see through it.

"A man came out of the fish pond!" Naomi wailed.

Another thud, and the door flew open.

A large bald man stepped through the threshold.

Boyd was a skeptic. He'd stopped believing in monsters hiding in the closet or lurking under his bed long before his childhood friends did. He didn't believe in aliens, or ESP, or any of that stuff that didn't have a solid scientific explanation. But when somebody broke into your home and you could see right through him...it was a fucking ghost.

Of course, ghosts weren't supposed to be able to open doors. He'd worry about that later.

Adeline, Paige, and Naomi all screamed. Boyd probably would have joined them if his voice was working.

The transparent man staggered forward. His eyes were wide with confusion and he acted like he couldn't breathe. He kicked the door shut behind him, revealing that the wood was almost completely rotten. He braced himself against the wall with one hand—the other stayed clutched to his throat—and continued slowly moving toward them.

"Get the girls out of the house," Boyd told Adeline, although as soon as he blurted out the words he realized that Adeline had already taken Paige and Naomi's hands and they were running toward the living room.

The transparent man lost his balance and fell to the floor.

Boyd would follow his wife and daughters. In a moment.

"Who the hell are you?" he demanded.

The man looked up at him and let out a soft choking noise.

"Are you a ghost?"

The man didn't answer. Using the wall for leverage, he began to pull himself back up.

The five seconds Boyd had allotted himself to investigate the mysteries of life after death were over. He turned and ran.

- - -

The door in the living room had rotted as well. All of

the windows were bubbled. Adeline couldn't believe that they'd thought their problems might have stemmed from an improperly vacuumed air duct.

The doorknob was covered with rust. Adeline grabbed it and cried out in pain; it felt like she'd slammed her hand against a cactus. She looked at her palm. It was covered with black marks.

She fought back tears of pain. She could focus on her hand later. For now, they had to get out of the house.

If Adeline weren't barefoot, she would've tried to kick the door. Instead of running back to the bedroom to get a pair of shoes (she suddenly wished they were a "take off your shoes as you walk into the house" kind of family) it would be much faster to let Boyd kick the door open. He should be here with them anyway.

"Boyd!" she shouted. "We need you!"

Boyd rushed into the living room. Clearly, he'd already been on his way.

"The doorknob bit my hand," said Adeline. She wasn't sure why she used the word "bit." It just came out without her thinking about it. "We need you to kick it open."

"I don't have my shoes on."

Crap, Adeline thought. Boyd didn't usually take off his shoes until he got undressed for bed. Nice day to mess with tradition.

Boyd walked over to the door. "I'll do it anyway."

"No, no—you'll break your foot!"

The man (the ghost?) stepped into the living room. He was no longer using the wall to keep himself upright, and his hand was no longer on his throat, though he still sounded and looked like he was choking.

"Get away from us," Boyd told the man. "Get the hell

out of our home."

The man cocked his head a bit, as if trying to understand what Boyd was saying to him.

"We're not going to hurt you," Boyd assured him.

It was difficult to gauge the man's facial expression, since his features weren't clear, but it sure seemed like he was amused by Boyd's statement. When he threw back his head and laughed, even while sounding as if he could barely breathe, there was no question about his reaction.

The living room didn't have much in the way of projectiles, but it did have a glass vase that would have contained flowers at some point in the future. Boyd picked it up and hurled it at the man with amazing accuracy, presuming that he'd been aiming at his chest and not his head.

The vase passed right through him. Not like air. More like jelly, losing its momentum after going through his body and shattering on the hardwood floor. Injuring the see-through man by throwing a vase had been a long shot, but he clearly wasn't immune to all of the laws of physics, so it had been worth a shot.

He looked down at his chest, as if surprised by what had happened.

Then, seemingly emboldened by this new information, he came at them, moving more quickly than before.

"Go! Go! Go!" shouted Boyd, grabbing Paige's hand while Adeline kept hold of Naomi's. The four of them rushed past the man back into the hallway. But before she could get completely out of his reach, the man grabbed Adeline by the wrist.

She expected the needles-through-the-skin sensation again and for a split-second she actually felt it, but no, it didn't feel *that* much different from a flesh-and-blood person's grip. She tried to tug her hand free. He wouldn't let go.

"*Mommy!*"

Adeline realized that she was still holding Naomi's hand and preventing her from running away with her father and sister. Adeline released her and then took a swing at the man. The vase hadn't hurt him, but a punch to the jaw might at least surprise him.

It felt like punching a wet towel. Her fist went through his head without shifting his features. The man opened his mouth wide, revealing transparent teeth, his face contorting with rage.

She couldn't tell if it hurt him or not. But when she yanked her hand again, her wrist popped free.

"Don't touch the doorknob!" Adeline screamed as she realized that Boyd was about to do just that. "Go in our bedroom!" Thank God it was a one-story house; they'd just climb out the window.

Boyd looked confused but didn't argue. He, Paige, and Naomi rushed into the bedroom. Adeline followed them. The door to the bedroom had no trace of the rot, so she pulled it shut behind her and locked it.

"What was that?" asked Paige, her hands trembling so violently that Adeline worried that she might further injure her eye.

"I don't know. But I don't think it can pass through doors, so it won't get us."

"I'll guard the door while you break the window," said Boyd.

Adeline nodded. The bed was pushed up against the window, so it would be difficult to open it (if it could be opened without a crowbar—it might've been painted shut). Adeline had no intention of wasting the time.

She opened the closet door and picked up a pair of red high heels. Then she climbed onto the bed, taking a moment to grab Boyd's cell phone off the bedstand and toss it to him. She tore down the blinds.

The window, like the windows in the living room and kitchen, looked like it was made out of boiling water, though the millions of tiny bubbles weren't moving.

"Stay back, honey," Adeline told Naomi. Naomi nodded and stepped away.

Adeline turned her head away from the window and then slammed one of her high heels against the glass. The window did not crack. It gave just a bit, as if she'd struck paste that had almost dried. The heel sunk about a quarter inch into the glass, leaving a small mark on the window and some sticky residue on the heel when she pulled it free.

"There's no reception," said Boyd. "No wireless and I'm not getting a single bar."

"How is that possible?" Adeline asked. It was a stupid question. If windows could transform their molecular structure and doorknobs could scar your hands, of course whatever was happening could block cell phone reception.

"I don't know!" said Boyd. He pulled Naomi and Paige in for a hug. "It'll be okay, I promise. Nothing's going to hurt you."

Adeline smacked the shoe against the window again, as hard as she could. The heel didn't go any further into the glass; all this accomplished was giving her a sharp pain in her shoulder. She tried to slide the heel down and dig a crevice into the glass, but it didn't work.

"I need something heavier," she told Boyd.

"Trade me spots," Boyd told her.

Adeline got off the bed and stood next to the door.

There was surprisingly little in their bedroom that could be used to break through a window. Boyd glanced around the room, then picked up the wooden bedstand and climbed up onto the mattress. He turned the bedstand upside-down, grabbed it by its legs, swung it back like a batter winding up for a home run, then smashed it into the glass.

The bedstand broke apart without damaging the window.

"Are you kidding me?" Boyd pressed the jagged end of one of the legs against the window, grunting with the strain, but it wouldn't puncture the glass. He tried Adeline's trick of using it as a digging tool. The best he could get was a light scrape across the surface.

The doorknob jiggled.

The ghost apparently couldn't pass through solid objects. That was good. As long as he couldn't pick a lock or break the door down, they'd be safe until help arrived. Not that they could call for help...

There was a *thump* on the other side of the door. Adeline clamped her uninjured hand over her mouth to block the scream.

Thump. Thump. Thump.

This was terrifying, but pounding on the door wasn't going to knock it off its hinges. They were fine. He couldn't get in.

Adeline could hear the choking noises through the door.

Boyd pulled his cell phone out of his pocket. "Paige, take this," he said. "Keep watching for a signal. Try moving around the room."

Paige nodded and took the phone from him.

Thump. Thump. Thump.

"Maybe we can melt the glass," said Boyd.

"With what?"

"We've got matches in the kitchen, right?"

"We're not in the kitchen!"

"I know we're not in the kitchen! I'm not saying it's our first choice! I'm throwing out ideas!"

"You're right, I'm sorry," said Adeline. They couldn't waste time fighting right now. If they escaped from this room but remained trapped in the house, melting the glass might indeed be their way out. Every idea had merit right now.

Thump.

This one was much louder and lower. The man was no longer pounding on the door; he was kicking it.

Boyd jumped off the bed and ran to the door. He pressed himself tightly against it as the kicks continued. Adeline pressed herself next to him.

"Anything?" Boyd asked Paige.

"No," she said, holding the phone high over her head.

The door shook so violently that Adeline thought it might have bruised her. This was, of course, in addition to the pain from the ice that hadn't yet faded, and the pain in her hand. Right now she was too frightened to really focus on it, but once they were out of this, she'd be in some serious discomfort.

Another kick and the lock broke.

One more kick and both Boyd and Adeline fell to the floor as the door burst open.

CHAPTER SIXTEEN

*B*oyd came inches from cracking his head against the bottom of the bedframe as he fell. The bedroom floor was carpeted (an ugly thin gray carpet that they would've replaced if they were buying the home instead of renting it) so the impact didn't hurt as much as it would have if they'd hit the hardwood floor elsewhere in the house. Still, though he was only thirty-two, Boyd was a bit too old to take a fall with grace.

The transparent man stood in the doorway for a moment. Then he lunged.

He went for Boyd. The man hovered over him, then crouched down and put his hands around Boyd's neck.

Boyd tried to tell Adeline to get the girls out of the room, but he couldn't breathe to speak. She either understood what he was trying to say or had the same idea on her own, because the three of them got the hell out of there.

The man's grip tightened. This close to him, Boyd could make out faint details he hadn't seen before—he could see the man's brain inside of his skull, and his internal organs inside his chest. Boyd attempted to grab the man's wrists and pull his hands away, but his hands passed through, ending up on his own neck. Apparently the ghost could touch but not be touched.

The man had a maniacal grin as he tried to strangle Boyd. A rope of drool dangled from the corner of his mouth but disappeared as soon as it fell.

Even for a guy who spent very little time contemplating his own mortality, Boyd never, ever considered that his demise might come at the hands of a homicidal ghost.

If he could talk, he'd try to reason with him. The ghost had to be here for some purpose aside from murdering the residents of the house, right? As it was, Boyd was not only unable to speak at the moment, but he was beginning to lose consciousness.

The man also continued to choke. His eyes were bulging slightly out of their sockets. What a horrific existence.

Boyd desperately used every bit of his strength to try to sit up, but no, the man held him down.

"Get the hell away from him!" Adeline shouted.

She had a large frying pan that she must've grabbed from the kitchen. She brought it down onto the man's head. It passed through, of course, and she stopped before it could smack into Boyd's face. Then she swung it back and forth, passing through the man's head over and over, apparently trying to distract him.

The man's grip didn't loosen.

Adeline switched tactics. She tossed the frying pan aside, grabbed Boyd's pants by the waist, and yanked him.

Boyd slid to the side, but not away from the man's chokehold.

Adeline yanked again.

That worked. It didn't feel like Boyd's neck popped free of the man's hands, but rather that it suddenly passed through them.

Boyd gasped for air. He was dizzy but there was no time for a recovery break. He got to his feet, as did the man, and followed Adeline out of the bedroom. Boyd pulled the door closed and held onto the doorknob with both hands.

"I can keep him in there!" said Boyd, though he may have missed a couple of words.

The doorknob immediately slipped out of his grip.

They ran into the kitchen.

"I found them!" said Paige, holding up a box of matches. She no longer had the cloth to her face, and her eye was caked with blood.

"See what you can do," Boyd told Adeline, and then he rushed at the man, passing through him. Though the man's body offered no resistance, Boyd immediately felt exhausted, drained. He lost his footing and fell onto the non-carpeted floor.

The man looked at him, then into the kitchen.

"Come and get me, you piece of shit!" Boyd said, scooting backwards and hoping that the man would consider him easier prey than two little girls.

The man took a step toward the kitchen.

"C'mon!" Boyd shouted. "Finish what you started!" He tried to think of a witty, devastating taunt but his mind was blank. He was lucky he could manage to call him a piece of shit.

The man seemed undecided for a moment, then went for Boyd.

This was what Boyd wanted, but his heart still gave a jolt.

- - -

The dishtowel that Adeline wrapped around the doorknob dropped to the floor in black, wet, steaming pieces that smelled the way she imagined a bloated corpse might reek when it split open inside the coffin.

Naomi was looking underneath the kitchen sink for a pair of rubber dish gloves. Adeline had taken out two frying pans before she went back to help Boyd, so she picked up the second one by the handle and went over to the door. Under normal circumstances nobody could bash through a door with a frying pan, but if it was rotted all the way through, this might work.

She took a swing, hitting it right in the center. The wood didn't give.

Half of the pan, suddenly covered with rust, crumbled away and fell to the floor as a powder.

Holy shit.

"I really need you to find those gloves!" she told Naomi. She snatched the box of matches out of Paige's hand. "Help your sister." Rubber gloves might not offer any more protection against the doorknob than the towel had, but if there was some kind of weird chemical reaction involved, they might.

Paige joined Naomi in the search.

Adeline slid open the box of matches and took out one of them as she crossed to the corner of the kitchen where the broom rested against the wall. She struck a match and held the flame to the broom fibers. They didn't catch. She kept the flame to the broom, expecting the ghost to burst into the kitchen at any moment. The broom stubbornly refused to ignite. People died every day from accidental fires, but she couldn't get a goddamn broom to catch fire on purpose.

Then it did.

She held the flaming broom against the glass. Having never melted glass before, she had no idea how long it would take to do this, but she wasn't trying to liquefy it, just soften it enough that she could poke through it. If the glass had the texture of paste, it might react like paste.

Nothing seemed to be happening.

"Is it working?" Boyd called out from the living room.

"Not yet!"

Paige triumphantly held up the dish gloves. "I found them!" The fact that Naomi didn't protest this victory was proof of how frightened she was.

Adeline kept the burning broom against the window, being careful not to ignite anything else in the process. "Hold onto them, sweetie," she said.

She needed Boyd here. No way in hell would she let Paige or Naomi get close to the door, but it was difficult to test this by herself. The glass didn't look any different, but maybe it was softer now and she just couldn't see it.

She carefully switched her grip to the center of the broomstick. Then she turned it around and pushed the non-burning end against the glass as hard as she could. No effect. She pounded the end of the broomstick against the window several times. The glass didn't crack.

Maybe the glass required more time to heat up. But there was only so long she could stand there holding a burning broom to the window.

- - -

The man followed Boyd into the living room. The

ghost had an advantage from the standpoint that it could hurt the living yet the living couldn't hurt him. But Boyd was faster, possibly because he wasn't constantly choking to death. He wondered if that was how the man died. There could, conceivably, be another explanation besides "spirit of a deceased man," but for now Boyd saw no reason to seek alternate theories. It was a ghost until he learned otherwise.

As long as he stayed on the move and didn't let himself get cornered, Boyd thought he could keep away from the ghost until Adeline figured out how to get them out of the house.

"Hey, dipshit! I'm right here! Show me what you can do!"

The man looked at him for a moment, then turned around.

Boyd suddenly feared that he'd overplayed his hand. If he made it too obvious that he wanted to keep the ghost focusing on him, the ghost—assuming it had the cognitive ability to make such decisions—might decide its attention was better off elsewhere.

Still, now that he'd screwed this up, he couldn't just let the ghost stroll off after his family.

He waved frantically. "Right here! I'm the one you want!" he said, knowing no such thing.

The ghost turned back to Boyd. It held up its hands and curled its fingers into claws.

Then it grinned and walked toward the kitchen.

– – –

Holding it by one of the fingers, Adeline swatted the rubber glove against the doorknob as she stomped on the broom that she'd dropped on the floor to extinguish the flames.

The glove, upon making contact, began to bubble and melt.

That there might be a logical scientific reason for what was happening in this house was always going to be a long shot, but this was the point where Adeline had to accept beyond any possible doubt that no researcher was going to be able to offer up a satisfactory explanation. They were in a haunted fucking house with an actual fucking ghost wandering around.

"Stay away from them!" she heard Boyd shout.

- - -

Boyd ran past the ghost. Adeline was in the kitchen holding an oozing rubber glove, so it was safe to say that they would not be exiting through the back door.

"Down in the basement!" he said.

Adeline didn't look like she agreed with that plan of action, and Boyd couldn't blame her. He'd thought it was a bad idea when he came up with it. With no cell phone reception and no expectation that help was on its way, trapping themselves in the basement sounded suicidal.

But, as Harry Cooper argued in *Night of the Living Dead*—and, ultimately, he'd been right in the basement vs. upstairs issue—it was only one door to guard. Granted, the same was true for any of the bathrooms or bedrooms in the house. What made the basement the best choice was that there was so much more room to maneuver. If the ghost kicked down the door, they could hide on the other end of the basement. When he walked over to them, they could (hopefully) get past him and back up the stairs without too much risk. Then maybe they could trap *him* down there.

There wasn't time to explain his full rationale, so he just said, "Trust me!"

Adeline opened the basement door and ushered Paige and Naomi down the stairs. Then she followed them, and Boyd took up the rear. He pulled the door closed, not bothering to lock it. The plan was for the ghost to follow them anyway.

He flipped on the light switch as Paige and Naomi reached the bottom of the stairs.

"Daddy's got this figured out," said Boyd. "If he comes down here, we can get around him, easy. We'll all run back upstairs, then we'll barricade the door with everything in the house, and he'll be stuck until help gets here."

"But we can't call the police," said Paige.

"I know, I know, but that doesn't mean nobody will ever come. Jack will come to check on us, at least."

"When?"

"It doesn't matter. If we trap the ghost down here, we can wait upstairs for as long as it takes."

"What if they can't get inside?" Naomi asked.

"We need to think positive right now," said Boyd, though the points his daughters were making were excellent ones. But even if every last scrap of food in the house rotted, they couldn't possibly be stuck here long enough to starve to death.

"Your father's right," said Adeline. "I know you're scared, but you won't have to be brave for much longer. Whatever that thing upstairs is, it's slow. It can't hurt us if it can't catch us, and we'll be too quick to catch."

Thump.

They all looked up at the door.

"This is fine," said Boyd. "This is what we want to happen. I don't think it can turn a knob, so we'll wait for it to kick the door open, if it even can, and then we'll all move to the back of the basement. Paige, you stick with Mom. I'll stay next to Naomi. We'll split up, and when I shout 'Go' we'll run back up the stairs. Everybody got it?"

Paige, Naomi, and Adeline all nodded.

Boyd took Naomi's hand. "Good. This will work. I promise."

Behind them, there was the sound of breaking glass—not a window, there were no windows down here—then the basement went dark.

"What happened?" asked Naomi, her voice cracking.

"The light bulb must've popped. It's okay. We're still okay."

They weren't *that* okay. Boyd's plan required them to actually be able to see the ghost. But when the door to upstairs came open, light from the kitchen would shine down, and maybe that would be enough.

The four of them stood in the darkness as the man kicked the door.

Thump. Thump. Thump.

Naomi cried softly. Boyd put his free hand on her shoulder.

He'd gotten away from the ghost when it had him pinned to the floor with its hands around his neck. Even in the dark, they could get away from it again, right?

That made complete sense, but Boyd's own words didn't reassure him.

Standing in a completely dark basement, with a monster kicking at the door, he couldn't truly believe that things were going to be all right.

He also, for a reason he couldn't quite explain, didn't feel that he and his family were alone in the basement.

Boyd didn't want to say anything, because surely it wasn't the truth, but he felt like something was behind them.

CHAPTER SEVENTEEN

*B*reathing.

Could he hear breathing?

No.

No, he couldn't.

That is, he *could*, but it was the others. The other living people. That's all it was. He was hearing the breathing of Adeline, Paige, and Naomi, not anything sinister.

The ghost continued to kick at the upstairs door.

Boyd turned his head, looking to the left and to the right, trying to be subtle.

"What's wrong?" asked Adeline.

"Nothing."

"Do you feel it too?"

"Feel what?" asked Paige.

"Just watch the door, honey."

"Are we alone down here?"

Should he lie? Boyd wanted to keep his daughters as calm as possible under the circumstances, not an easy task when those circumstances involved being in a dark basement with a ghost trying to force its way downstairs. But he also didn't want them to *not* speak up if they thought something was already down here with them.

He settled for saying, "I think so." At this point, how much more spooked could they get?

Thump. Thump. Thump.

The lock on the door to the basement seemed to be sturdier than the one to their bedroom. Maybe the ghost wouldn't be able to kick it open.

Thump. Thump. Thump.

The kicks didn't sound like they were getting more powerful. And since the ghost presumably couldn't use tools, it might have no way of coming after them. They might be safe down here.

Thump.

The door popped ajar.

Very slowly, with a creak—of course there was a creak, even though Boyd hadn't noticed the sound any of the other times he'd used this door—the basement door swung open. Light spilled down the stairs. The ghost stood in the doorway, motionless, staring down at them.

Naomi whimpered.

Boyd glanced around, trying to see if the light illuminated something frightening around them. He couldn't see anything. This was slightly reassuring, although there wasn't much light.

From this far away, it was impossible to discern the ghost's facial expression, but Boyd was pretty sure the goddamn thing was smiling at them. And it continued to choke.

It took a step down the stairs. Even though he'd heard it pounding on and kicking doors, Boyd was still surprised that its footstep made a sound. Then it took another very slow step. It made sense that if the ghost wasn't used to going down stairs, it would move slowly and tentatively, but that didn't appear to be the case. This seemed like a purposeful attempt to be intimidating.

The four of them backed up as the ghost went down another step.

Something moved behind them.

Boyd spun around. His imagination was going insane right now, but he didn't think he'd hallucinated the movement.

"What did you see?" asked Adeline.

"I don't know."

Should they stick to the plan? Boyd did not relish the idea of moving further back into the basement without knowing what the hell was down there with them. Maybe the four of them should just charge at the ghost.

No. It was a solid plan. If they rushed past (or through) the ghost, they might not be able to get the door closed in time to trap it. Until they had proof that something dangerous was down here, they needed to not panic. They'd be fine. Perfectly fine.

The ghost took another step down. That son of a bitch was definitely trying to scare them.

Boyd hoped that its constant choking put it in excruciating agony.

Paige cried out in surprise. "Something touched me!"

Boyd turned toward her, and another transparent man was *right the fuck there.*

Unlike the large man on the stairs, this ghost was almost freakishly skinny. Its head, inches away from Boyd's, tilted to the right. Too far to the right, as if it weren't completely attached.

Boyd instinctively moved away from the ghost. When it reached for him, he saw that its arms weren't completely attached either. There was a gap of a few inches at its shoulders, with its arms connected to its body with what appeared to be translucent red goo. The same goo connected its head to its neck. The ghost looked like it had been dismembered and then glued back together.

It grabbed Boyd's shirt.

The first ghost now stood at the bottom of the stairs, arms folded over its chest, blocking the way back up.

Naomi screamed.

Boyd pulled away from the ghost and his shirt tore free. He almost lost his footing but managed to stay upright. The ghost grabbed for him again, the ooze stretching, extending its reach.

Adeline screamed. Since the dismembered ghost's attention was on Boyd, there had to be another one of them down here.

The definition of insanity was doing the same thing and expecting a different result, but this was a different ghost, and perhaps they didn't all follow the same rules. Boyd threw a punch at the dismembered ghost's face. If it were human, this punch would've knocked out its front teeth. Instead, Boyd's fist passed harmlessly through its jaw. Boyd immediately felt as if he'd been going at a punching bag for several minutes, and, exhausted, he let his arm fall to his side.

The ghost grabbed him by the shoulders. Its head flopped forward, mouth wide open, and its teeth sunk into his cheek. It felt exactly like a real person biting his cheek.

Adeline pulled Naomi toward the stairs. "Run through it!" she shouted.

"I'm scared!"

"Run through it! I'll be right behind you!"

Naomi didn't move. Adeline pulled their daughter over

to the stairs and then shoved her forward. She passed through the first ghost and then tumbled onto the stairs.

"Run! Run!" Adeline shouted.

Naomi looked as if she were trying to get up, but couldn't summon the strength.

The ghost twisted around and grabbed a handful of her long black hair.

Boyd pulled away from the dismembered ghost. The translucent red goo connecting its head to its neck stretched even further and its teeth remained in Boyd's face. He could feel trickles of blood running down his cheek.

The ghost on the stairs yanked Naomi to her feet.

"Go through!" Adeline told Paige. Without hesitation, Paige ran through the ghost, colliding with Naomi. They both fell. Several strands of black hair floated in the ghost's fist.

Boyd caught a glimpse of a third ghost, right next to Adeline.

Paige shrieked as the staircase ghost grabbed her hair.

Adeline pushed through it. Now all three of them were lying on the stairs in a pile, drained, but this broke its grip on Paige's hair, apparently without ripping out a blonde curl.

Boyd's arm was already regaining its strength, so hopefully the girls would recover quickly. He didn't know if the dismembered ghost's head could stretch to cartoonish lengths, and he didn't want to test it out. If he pulled too hard, it might take a huge chunk of his face with it.

He felt something between its teeth. Something cold and slimy. A tongue.

The ghost was licking him while it was biting him.

If it was trying to freak him out, well done. Boyd was thoroughly freaked out.

The ghost on the stairs reached down and this time it grabbed both Adeline's and Paige's hair. It yanked both of their heads back. Boyd prayed it didn't have the power to break their necks.

Naomi scrambled out from underneath them and hurried up the stairs.

The dismembered ghost opened its mouth, releasing Boyd. Apparently it just wanted to get in another bite, because it lunged for him again. This time, when Boyd pulled out of the way, he did lose his footing, and fell to the cement floor.

The third ghost walked toward him.

There wasn't enough light to get a good look at this one, but its skin—if you could call it skin—was a lot different. It was an uneven mix of reds and purples, with grotesque swelling in some areas. It looked like somebody who'd lost a fight against ten other guys.

Now Paige went up the stairs. The ghost followed her, leaving Adeline behind.

The idea of trapping one ghost in the basement was now abandoned, the product of a simpler, more innocent time in Boyd's life. At this point, he just needed to get out of here.

Adeline let out a wail of fury; a mother whose children were in danger. But it was clear that she was still too weak to go after the ghost.

The bruised ghost crouched down next to Boyd. Unlike the others, it didn't appear to be enjoying this experience. Its face was a scowl of pure hatred. The degree of loathing in its expression would've been scary as hell if Boyd saw it on a regular human being, much less something supernatural.

Boyd scooted away from it.

Maybe it couldn't see in the dark.

He kept going. This was taking him away from the stairs to safety, but if it meant that Adeline and the girls only had to contend with one ghost instead of three, it was worth the danger. And, indeed, the dismembered ghost and the bruised ghost moved his way until they were lost in the darkness.

Adeline turned around, obviously trying to see what was happening to him.

"I'll be fine!" Boyd shouted. "Keep the girls safe!"

Adeline looked heartsick over the idea of leaving him behind, but when their daughters were in immediate peril, there was really no choice. She hurried up the stairs. The ghost was almost at the top. Adeline stopped behind it, most likely deciding that having her strength drained by passing through its body would defeat the purpose of getting ahead of it.

The ghost realized she was right behind it. It spun around and grabbed Adeline's face.

Then it shoved her.

She didn't do a complete backwards drop, which almost certainly would have broken her spine and snapped her neck. She was able to twist around, tumbling sideways, and grabbed at the wooden railing. Though she wasn't able to hold on to it, it helped break her fall.

But she still fell hard, bouncing twice on the way down. And when she struck the floor at the bottom, she didn't get back up.

The ghost stepped into the kitchen, then kicked the door shut.

Seeing his wife injured (*killed?*) was enough to

overwhelm Boyd's emotions so that for a moment he didn't even think about being stuck in complete darkness with a pair of ghosts. When he did process the situation, he focused less on his terror and more on the need to get Adeline to safety. Though there was still plenty of terror.

She's not dead she can't be dead there's just no way she's dead.

Boyd got up.

Something sliced across the back of his arm, elbow to wrist. He didn't think it cut him too deep, but it stung like hell.

Did the ghosts have weapons now?

He always rolled his eyes in movies when characters said, "What do you want from me?" But now that he was fighting monsters with unknown motives, it was, in fact, a very good fucking question.

"What do you want from me?"

The ghosts did not respond.

He could hear footsteps moving away from him, almost definitely toward Adeline's fallen body.

Then heard the patter of something dripping on the floor. He touched his arm. He'd been wrong; the cut was deep and bleeding badly.

Something stabbed into his left thigh.

It felt like a knife, plunging in all the way to the hilt. He didn't want to frighten Naomi and Paige, but it was the worst pain he'd ever experienced in his life, and he couldn't stop the scream.

It hurt almost as much when it was wrenched out.

The door upstairs slowly began to swing open.

Boyd staggered toward the stairs. The ghosts were slow. Even with a bloody hole in his leg, he could escape them. He just needed Adeline to wake up.

The door continued opening. He didn't see anybody

doing it. It was probably swinging open on its own; a result of the damage from the ghost breaking the lock.

With the light, he could see that Adeline remained motionless on the floor. He could see a thin line of blood running from the side of her mouth all the way down to her ear.

Something stabbed into the back of his left arm, going so deep that it hit bone.

He spun around as the weapon was yanked out of his flesh.

The bruised ghost was right behind him. It wasn't holding a knife. In fact, it wasn't holding anything. How had it stabbed him?

It held up its arm. A jagged bone, the radius, broke through the skin.

The ghost lunged forward with the bone. Boyd was almost too shocked to move, but he stepped back in time to narrowly avoid having the broken bone plunge into his chest.

The bone disappeared back into the ghost's arm, and the wound sealed up.

The ghost held up its other arm. It seemed to be gritting its teeth, bracing itself for the intense pain. Another jagged bone burst through its arm. A flap of transparent flesh dangled from the tip.

Boyd knew he should run—not that he'd be able to run very well after getting stabbed in the thigh—but he was stuck on trying to comprehend what he was seeing. You had to really, *really* want to harm somebody to purposely let a broken bone rip through your skin.

Blood dripped from the ghost's arm. Boyd couldn't see the basement floor clearly enough to know if it left a trace.

The dismembered ghost grabbed Boyd's shoulder. It should have been too far away to reach him, so Boyd had the red ooze connecting its limbs to thank. It pulled Boyd closer to the bruised ghost, who immediately crouched down and stabbed him in the leg.

Boyd jerked himself away, snapping off the bone. The ghost let out a shriek of agony; the intensity was clear but it didn't make much sound, like a heavy metal album played at low volume.

The bone faded away.

Somehow Boyd hadn't fallen over again, though it was clear that if he did escape, he'd be crawling, not walking. He looked over at Adeline. She was still unconscious. God, he hoped she was just unconscious...

The bruised ghost had recovered quickly from its pain. Its expression was back to pure rage. It stood up and stretched its arms out to the sides. It was breathing deeply, apparently psyching itself up for what was about to happen.

Several broken rib bones burst through its chest.

Boyd's legs finally gave out. He hit the floor, landing in his own blood.

The ghost looked down, as if horrified by the sight of its mangled torso. Then it returned its attention to Boyd. As Boyd frantically tried to scoot away, the ghost walked over to him, and then dropped to its knees.

CHAPTER EIGHTEEN

A deline opened her eyes at the sound of Boyd's scream.

She remembered exactly where she was and what had happened, so the ghosts were not a surprise. She was not, however, expecting to see broken rib bones protruding from one of their chests, or for the ghost to be hovering over Boyd as if preparing to give him an innards-mangling horizontal hug.

The other ghost noticed that she was conscious and walked toward her, moving like somebody who was still getting used to how his arms and legs worked. Its head swayed with each step, almost threatening to flop backwards.

Adeline stood up.

The split-ribcage ghost noticed her as well.

It was only distracted for a moment, but that was enough time for Boyd to scoot away some more, leaving a trail of blood. The ghost crawled after him.

The other ghost reached for Adeline. It was much too far away to actually grab her...but the red ooze connecting its limbs to its body stretched like cheese on a pizza. It should have looked silly, and if she were a casual observer rather than the person the severed arm was stretching toward, it might have. But right now, in this moment, it did not look silly at all.

"Go help the girls!" Boyd shouted. "Don't worry about me!"

The ghost raked its broken bones over Boyd's leg as it crawled on top of him.

The dismembered ghost's arm dropped to the floor right before it reached the staircase. So the ooze didn't stretch forever, but the ghost still had a good ten-foot reach. It gave a tug with its shoulder, and its arm snapped back into place. Mostly; the limb still hung almost to the floor.

"I said go! I'm okay!"

Boyd was most assuredly *not* okay, not with a ghost about to jam its entire broken ribcage into his chest. The choking ghost was upstairs with Paige and Naomi, and Adeline was terrified for their safety, but she was going to sacrifice ten seconds to get Boyd out of immediate danger.

She ran over to Boyd and grabbed him by the underarms. She dragged him out of the way *almost* in time to save him from the rib bones cutting into his belly. He had several deep gashes and a ruined shirt, but at least he hadn't been disemboweled.

The ghost grabbed Boyd's foot before he could slide completely out of the way.

Adeline yanked hard, and Boyd's foot popped out of the ghost's grasp. She hurriedly dragged him to the stairs.

"Can you walk?" she asked.

"Don't worry about me. I'll get up there. Leave me here, please!"

Adeline couldn't spare any more time. She had to

make sure their daughters were safe. There wasn't even time to give Boyd a kiss, so she ran up the stairs. "I'm coming back for you!" she promised. She wanted to tell him that she loved him, but "I love you" felt like final words, an acknowledgement that she might be leaving her husband to die. So she didn't say them.

She ran into the kitchen, which was empty.

At the far end of the hallway, she saw the choking ghost.

"Hey!" she shouted.

The ghost turned toward her.

Adeline ran halfway down the hallway. As far as she knew, she still had a speed advantage, so she could get relatively close to the ghost as she tried to lure it away. She wanted to call out to the girls, but also didn't want them to give away their hiding spot if they'd found one.

The ghost stepped out of sight.

"Come and get me!" Adeline shouted. "I'm the one you want!"

Presumably she was not the one it wanted, because the ghost did not return to the hallway. Cautiously but quickly, Adeline walked to the end of the hallway.

The ghost stood underneath the trapdoor to the attic. It swiped at the cord but its hand passed harmlessly through it. The ghosts were good at kicking and pounding, but not at things like working doorknobs or pulling cords.

Adeline didn't like the idea of the girls being trapped anywhere, but it honestly seemed like the most secure place to be. If Paige and Naomi were safe in the attic, Adeline could go back and help Boyd, and then maybe try to get up there with their daughters until help arrived.

The ghost swiped again. The cord swayed a bit.

Maybe that didn't mean anything. Maybe the air conditioner was blowing on it.

One more swipe. The cord swung. There was no way to blame this on anything except the ghost getting better at object manipulation. How long until it could actually yank on the cord? Could it then lower the folded ladder? How much danger were Paige and Naomi in if she abandoned them right now?

The ghost got a hold of the cord. It yanked, but though the cord jiggled, its hand passed through before it could actually open the door.

Adeline wished there was something she could do to *hurt* the ghost. What kind of weakness could it possibly have? How could she stop it if everything passed harmlessly through its body?

Oh, sure, it was conceivable that it did have a weakness, like silver or sunlight or prayer, but how the hell would she ever discover that? Just start throwing everything in the house at it and hope that something revealed its one hidden vulnerability, like a video game character?

The ghost was still choking.

Its face was bloated.

Drowning?

It might have a ghostly chicken bone stuck in its throat, but it could also be forever drowning. How would something that was stuck in an eternal loop of drowning react to water?

Adeline darted past the ghost into the bathroom. She turned on the faucet and cupped her hands under the water. When they were full to overflowing, she stepped out of the bathroom and flung the water in its face.

The water passed through and splashed onto the floor.

The ghost turned to look at her. It didn't speak, but its expression read *What the hell was that supposed to be, lady?*

Okay, the ghost did not have a magical vulnerability to water. Duly noted.

It tugged on the cord, and the trapdoor popped open.

Adeline shoved the trapdoor back up.

The ghost punched her in the face. Adeline struck the wall, then fell to the floor, blood filling her mouth. She hadn't just bitten her tongue; she'd taken off a piece of the side. A front tooth may have been knocked loose.

She stood back up as the ghost lowered the trapdoor again.

It would be an unfair fight even if they were both flesh and blood. Since it could hit her but she couldn't hit it back, fighting it was impossible. Her only choice was to get into the attic first and keep it out.

Paige peeked down. "*Mom!*"

"It's okay, honey! I'm coming!"

Adeline could definitely climb a ladder faster than the ghost. But she'd have to pass through it first, and that came with a huge energy drain. So she'd have to hope that she could beat the ghost up there even in a weakened state. Since this goddamn ghost was standing between a mother and her children, Adeline was confident that she'd win the race.

She moved away from the ladder, into Naomi's bedroom, to get a running start.

The ghost took a wobbly step onto the first rung of the ladder.

Adeline sprinted for the ladder.

She passed through the ghost and instantly felt faint, yet scrambled up most of the way. She collapsed as she grabbed the top rung. But she fell forward instead of backward and kept her spot on the ladder.

Paige reached down and grabbed Adeline's arm. "Help me!" Paige told Naomi, who reached down and grabbed her other arm. The ghost, meanwhile, grabbed her foot.

Adeline had to call up every last reserve of strength. She wasn't going to be pulled down the ladder (or, worse, torn in half between the two) when she was this close to getting to her daughters.

She violently shook her leg to get it free while Paige and Naomi tried to pull her up.

This would be so much easier if she could just kick the ghost in the face.

Naomi was losing her grip.

Then Adeline's foot came free. She ran up the rest of the ladder, then turned around, grabbed the top rung, and started to pull it up. The ghost was on the ladder but had no weight, so there was no resistance. Was it going to be pulled right up into the attic with her?

When the ladder started to fold, Adeline released it. It fell back to the floor. Unfortunately, the impact was gentle and didn't knock off the ghost.

She pulled up the ladder again, bringing the ghost with it.

This time, when she released it, she used her feet to give the ladder more momentum. It slammed against the floor. The ghost didn't fall, but it did put its arms out for balance and step off the ladder. Adeline pulled the ladder up again. The ghost quickly grabbed for the ladder, and its arms passed right through.

Adeline pulled the ladder all the way up, closing the trapdoor.

One of the girls had turned on the light, but the attic was still eerie, illuminated only by a single weak bulb.

Paige and Naomi both threw their arms around Adeline. She wanted to tell them that she loved them and reassure them that everything was going to be all right, but she thought her words would lose their ability to soothe if blood spewed out of her mouth while she spoke them.

She turned away and spat the blood onto some fiberglass insulation.

"Are you hurt?" Paige asked. A lot more blood had soaked through the washcloth she held over her eye.

"I'm fine. Don't worry about me." Adeline wiped her mouth with the back of her hand.

"Where's Dad?"

"He's also fine." Maybe this was the truth. Maybe it was a lie. Either way, the girls didn't need to know that their father was badly injured in the basement with the ghosts.

"Can it get up here?" asked Naomi.

"It's not good at it, but it can pull the cord. I think I'll be able to hold the door shut."

"I didn't want to trap us up here, but there was nowhere else to go," said Paige.

"No, no, you did the right thing. If you shut yourself in a closet there'd be no way to escape. If it gets up here, we can still get away."

"How?" asked Naomi.

Adeline hesitated. It wasn't a *good* escape plan.

"I'm going to need you to crawl over those planks," said Adeline, pointing to her left. "All the way to the wall. You're going to wait there while I guard the trapdoor."

"It can still come after us there," said Paige.

Adeline shook her head. "If you go where I direct you, you'll be right over the couch. If you have to—and I'm sure you won't, but if you *have* to—you can break through the ceiling and you'll land on the cushions."

Paige frowned. "Are you sure you know exactly where the couch is?"

Adeline decided not to lie. "I'm pretty sure. Ninety percent."

Paige and Naomi looked at each other. She expected them to protest. Instead, Naomi gave a solemn nod. "Okay."

"Do it now. You go first, Paige."

It wasn't safe for them to be crawling across the narrow beams, and the girls might be taking an unnecessary risk if the ghost never did get up here. But the light bulb in the basement had shattered, and if the same happened to the attic bulb they'd be crawling in the darkness, which would be infinitely more dangerous. Better to do it while they still had light.

Paige, more fearless than Adeline would have thought, began to crawl along the beam. She moved quickly, pausing only to brush a cobweb out of her face. Within a few moments she was on the other side of the attic, right above where Adeline hoped the living room couch rested.

"Your turn," Adeline told Naomi.

"What if I fall off?"

"You won't."

"But what if I do?"

"You're tiny," said Adeline. "You won't break through. It'll be okay. Just crawl over to Paige."

There was a thump on the other side of the trapdoor. Naomi screamed.

"Go!" said Adeline.

Naomi crawled out onto the beam, far more tentatively than Paige had done. Adeline wanted her to hurry, but didn't want to *urge* her to hurry; if Naomi got too scared and slipped off the beam, she might very well break through the ceiling and crash onto the hardwood floor below.

"C'mon!" said Paige. "It's easy! The wood is sturdy. Nothing's going to happen to you."

Naomi kept crawling, slowly but steadily.

"See how easy this is?" asked Paige. "You're doing great!"

"Be quiet!" said Naomi. "You're making me nervous!"

Paige stopped offering moral support.

The ghost kept pounding, and the trapdoor shook with each blow, but the impact wasn't nearly enough to knock Adeline aside. If she stayed in place, in theory the ghost couldn't pound its way into the attic.

When Naomi was halfway across, Adeline noticed a shadow falling across the beams.

No, not a shadow.

The wood was discoloring.

Rotting.

CHAPTER NINETEEN

*B*oyd dragged himself up the stairs, leaving a significant amount of blood behind. He couldn't figure out why the ghosts were letting him get away.

Just as his hand clutched the very top step, one of the ghosts grabbed his foot and pulled him all the way back down the stairs. His chin struck one of the stairs so hard that he thought he split it wide open.

The ghosts laughed.

Great, they could laugh now.

"*Go kill...*" said the bruised ghost. The sentence stopped as if its mouth went dry. "*Go kill his family.*" Its voice had a distant sound, like it was coming from another room, and it was like two recordings of the same person played almost simultaneously but just a split second off.

The dismembered ghost, whose arms had retracted most of the way, went up the stairs and into the kitchen.

The bruised ghost sat on the bottom stair. It raised its right hand in a fist. A transparent bone ripped through the skin of its index finger, and it held up the bone to Boyd's eye.

"*Wanna look like your daughter?*" it asked.

185

Boyd moved his head out of the way.

"*Relax,*" said the ghost. "*I can't be that precise. I'd just poke your eye out.*"

"Leave my family alone," said Boyd.

"*Why tell me? I'm not the one going after them. You're talking to the wrong person. My attention is on you.*" It gently dragged the index finger bone across the back of Boyd's neck. "*My complete, undivided attention.*"

Then it jabbed the bone into Boyd's shoulder, all the way to the second knuckle. Boyd screamed and twisted away.

"*Hurts, huh? Hurts me, too. Worth it, though.*"

"What the fuck do you want?" Boyd asked.

"*Do you kiss your daughters with that mouth?*"

"I asked you a question!"

The ghost smiled. The index finger bone curled back into its fist. "*Trying to be a tough guy? I respect that. Respect the hell out of that. If I were as deeply screwed as you, I'd probably be sobbing and begging for my life.*"

Boyd didn't want to admit to himself how close he was to reaching that point. He didn't see a way out of this.

"You still haven't answered," he said, trying to sound a million times braver than he actually felt.

The ghost held up its other fist. An index finger broke through, and it jabbed it deep into Boyd's other shoulder, giving him identical flowing wounds.

"*We're taking your energy,*" said the ghost. "*Guess how we do that?*"

"I don't know."

"*Guess.*"

"Killing us?"

"*Yes indeed. Slowly and horribly. We sucked away energy to cross over, and now we're going to drain your energy to stay over. You picked the wrong house."*

"What does it mean to take our energy? Why did Paige cut herself?"

"I'm not here to answer your questions. I'm happy for you to die confused."

A bone broke through its arm.

"How many holes do you think I can poke in you before you die? Twenty? Fifty? A hundred? I hope it's a hundred."

"Just kill me," said Boyd. "Leave my family alone."

"Ooooh, we would if we could. Do you think we want to murder innocent little girls? I also hate the idea of killing that hot piece of ass who's out of your league. What a waste. But you've gotta do what you've gotta do. If we had another option, we'd take it. Unfortunately for you and your precious family, we don't."

Boyd wondered how long it would take him to bleed out. He had deep puncture wounds in one arm, one leg, and each shoulder, plus slashes all over both legs and his stomach, and what felt like a nasty gash on his chin. He might be okay. He'd watched action movie heroes walk away from worse.

Of course, he wasn't an action hero, and he wasn't in a movie, and he was just trying to distract himself from the knowledge that he might very well be dying, and that Adeline, Paige, and Naomi might not survive to nightfall. They could be dead already. Adeline could be watching their children die while Boyd lay on the stairs, bleeding.

He felt like he could summon a burst of strength, but what good would that do? Get him to the top of the stairs in time to be dragged back down again?

How could he get the upper hand against a ghost he couldn't touch? What could he do? Appeal to its sense of decency?

"You should probably try to think of a happy memory, since you aren't going to make any more of them," said the ghost. *"It's nothing but suffering for you until everything goes black."*

Boyd wanted to punch the ghost, even though it would have no impact, just to prove that his spirit wasn't broken. But he also wanted to be smart, so he didn't.

He wiped his chin off on his sleeve. There was even more blood than he'd expected. "At least tell me your name. I like to know who's killing me."

"Maddox."

"Decent name."

"Let's get back to the holes. I'm going to fill you with holes, Boyd. Lots of tiny little holes until you wouldn't recognize yourself in a mirror. If I had a needle, I bet I could keep you alive for days. Fortunately for you, I have to be a little sloppier."

The ghost held up its fist again. This time all five of the finger bones burst out of the skin.

"Where should we start?"

"Go to Paige!" Adeline shouted. "Hurry! As fast as you can!"

Naomi picked up her pace as the wooden floor of the attic continued to fill with splotches of black and dark green. The rotting smell was sickening.

A can of paint broke through the wood and plummeted below, landing with a crash.

Adeline wanted to crawl over to Paige as well, but the wood was decomposing so quickly that she didn't think she'd make it in time. Better to fall here, where she might be able to grab the ladder on the way down, than to drop to the center of the living room.

Paige extended her hand toward Naomi, who was still about ten feet away. "Hurry, Naomi, please!"

Naomi's hand broke through the beam and she froze.

Adeline looked up. If the roof were rotting, it could give them some sort of escape route, but no, of course the roof was fine and they were still trapped.

Paige started to crawl toward her sister. Her hand sunk into the beam as if it were thick oatmeal.

"Naomi, stand up!" said Adeline. "Grab the roof beams!"

Though Naomi could be forgiven if she'd stayed in place, frozen with terror, she immediately stood up and grabbed one of the wooden beams attached to the attic roof. Naomi was good on the jungle gym. Maybe she could hang on long enough for them to move the couch underneath her.

The wood beneath Adeline began to transform.

Naomi, demonstrating an eight-year-old girl's gift for gymnastics, pulled herself all the way up onto the beam and draped her legs over it. As long as that wood didn't rot away, she wasn't going to fall.

The floor beneath Paige collapsed. She disappeared with a shriek.

There was no *thump* or *crunch* or any sound to indicate that Paige had missed the couch. She was okay. She had to be.

The attic floor was almost completely rotten now, a pool of black and green and mildew-gray. "We'll get you down," Adeline promised Naomi.

Instead of waiting to break through, Adeline decided that she should just open the trap door and climb down. She tugged on the metal handle and it popped right off. She could, in theory, lift it by the sides, but touching the liquefying wood didn't seem like a good idea.

She was sinking through. She positioned herself directly over the ladder and waited.

The entire ceiling collapsed.

It all came down in a thick shower of rotted wood, plaster, insulation, and electrical wiring. Adeline hit the ladder, bashing her knees hard but keeping her from falling all the way to the floor. She grabbed the top rung as debris rained upon her.

Then she realized that she was inside of the choking ghost. She felt faint and slipped off the ladder, landing in a pile of rubble.

- - -

Boyd and the bruised ghost both looked up at the enormous crash.

What the hell was that?

The distraction didn't last long. The ghost jabbed another broken bone into his back.

- - -

"Mom!" shouted Paige.

Adeline lifted her head. Paige had indeed landed on the couch, thank God.

The choking ghost was climbing down the ladder toward Adeline.

The dismembered ghost was walking toward Paige. But maneuvering around the rubble was apparently as difficult for a ghost as it would be for a human.

Adeline checked to see that Naomi was still safely perched up in the attic. Unfortunately, moving her head was all she could manage. The rest of her body remained devoid of strength.

Paige got up off the couch. She'd dropped the washcloth, revealing caked blood over her eye. She scrambled over the wreckage of the ceiling toward Adeline. The dismembered ghost reached for her.

The choking ghost skipped the last couple of rungs and jumped down, its feet landing on each side of Adeline's prone body. This would be the perfect opportunity for her to punch the ghost in the balls, if her hand wouldn't pass harmlessly through them.

The dismembered ghost's arm stretched out and it grabbed Paige by the hair. She frantically tried to pull away but its grip was too tight. It began to drag her toward it.

The choking ghost crouched down over Adeline, grabbed her by the hair as well, and slammed her head into the floor.

"Mommy!" Naomi screamed.

The doorbell rang.

CHAPTER TWENTY

"What took you so long?" Donna asked the police officer as he got out of his car. "They've been screamin' in there like crazy."

"I was dispatched as soon as your call was received," said the officer.

"Well, there was just a crash like the whole damn house caved in. I don't know if he's beatin' on her or if it's a meth lab or what they've got goin' on, but these new neighbors are out of control."

"Thank you for alerting us. You can return to your home now."

"No way. I want to see what's going on."

The police officer walked up to the front door, then turned back to look at Donna. "How old is this house?"

"The door wasn't like that before. I'm tellin' you, these new folks are maniacs. They haven't even been here a week and the place looks like it's been abandoned for years. And it reeks. You smell that?"

"I certainly do."

"You're gonna kick 'em out, right?"

"I'm going to find out why they were screaming and deal with it appropriately."

The police officer rang the doorbell.

- - -

Adeline had no idea who was at the door, but she suddenly realized that they were in danger even if they didn't come inside.

"Don't touch the door!" she shouted. The ghost bashed her head into the floor again. "Paige, tell them not to touch the door!"

- - -

Officer Peter Farlind stepped away from the door as a woman, and then a girl shouted for him not to touch it. If they hadn't sounded so frantic, he might have thought they were warning him not to touch wet paint. But something was obviously deeply wrong at this house.

"This is the police," he announced. "We received a call about a disturbance."

"Yes!" the girl inside said. "There's a disturbance! But don't touch the door!"

Somebody else said something that Peter couldn't quite make out.

"That's right, there's contamination!" said the girl. "Don't touch the door!"

Contamination? There was no green glow, but the house sure looked like something that had been too close to a nuclear power plant.

He pulled his walkie-talkie off his belt and called for backup. Even if this whole thing was a weird prank, he wanted somebody else to see it.

"You need to get us out of here!" the girl shouted.

"Please help us!"

Peter glanced back at the middle-aged woman who'd called the cops. "Ma'am, I'm going to need you to clear the area. I don't think it's safe here."

The woman took several steps back but didn't leave.

The window next to the front door was completely fogged up. Well, no, not fogged; it was filled with so many tiny bubbles that he couldn't see through it. Strange.

Under normal circumstances, "contamination" would have meant "leave it alone and contact the experts." But if people, including a child, were in imminent danger, he had to try and get them out before it was too late.

He quickly took off his shirt while the woman stared at him. He wrapped it over his nose and mouth, figuring it was better than nothing if a cloud of gas bellowed out of the window, and then kicked the glass.

His foot bounced back and he almost toppled over.

He kicked again. Nothing. It was less like glass than really thick rubber.

Peter took his gun out of its holster. "Ma'am, I'm not going to tell you again to leave. If this bullet ricochets, you don't want to be here."

"Please help us!" the girl inside screamed.

The woman turned and ran.

"Make sure nobody is near the window," said Peter. "I'm going to shoot through the glass. Do you understand?"

"Yes, yes! Shoot the glass!"

Peter waited for the woman to get out of possible harm's way. He stepped to the side so that a ricochet wouldn't fly back at him, aimed his gun, and squeezed the trigger.

The bullet left a small round hole.

Then the glass oozed over the hole, sealing it off.

In his seventeen years as a cop, Peter had never encountered anything like this. He should wait for backup.

"Please!" the girl screamed.

Or he should take more drastic measures.

"Stay clear of this wall," he said. "Do you hear me? Make sure you're nowhere near this wall!"

"Okay!" said the girl.

Again, under normal circumstances, Peter would *never* consider driving his car through the wall of a house. And if the people inside were messing with him, he'd be the laughingstock of the entire department. But they certainly didn't sound like they were kidding around, and you had to really be invested in a practical joke to let it continue past the point where a police officer told you to stay away from your wall.

He got into his car, started the engine, backed up a few feet, then turned the vehicle so that it was facing the front of the house. He buckled his seatbelt, took a deep breath, and floored the gas pedal.

A second before impact, he wondered if he was behaving in too impulsive a manner.

The police car broke through the front of the house. Peter slammed on the brakes as half of the vehicle passed through the wall. That worked better than he'd expected. Now he just needed to put the car in reverse and...

Jesus Christ. What had happened in here?

The entire ceiling had collapsed. A little girl, seven or eight years old, was hanging up in the rafters. A teenaged girl was pressed against the far wall. A woman was on the floor.

Also there were...no, Peter was hallucinating. You didn't perceive the world correctly in the seconds immediately after driving your car through the front of somebody's home.

A few drops of liquid landed on the top of his head.

He looked up. The top of his car was leaking. There was no actual crack in the roof of the vehicle, but thick black liquid was dripping from it. Oil? Could he just not see how it was getting in?

The leak abruptly switched from a drip to a waterfall.

Peter was completely drenched. For a moment, he was too shocked to realize that it was beginning to burn.

The smell was noxious beyond belief, like an outhouse that had been storing food waste in triple-degree heat.

He reached for the gearshift, then screamed at the sight of muscles and tendons. He only saw them for a moment; then it was just bone.

The teenaged girl gaped at him in horror.

Peter's skeletal fingers fell off as he tried and failed to put the car into reverse. His right leg separated from the rest of his body and slid off the seat onto the floor of the car. His left leg followed. His torso flopped over.

He continued to scream until his tongue dropped out of his mouth.

- - -

"We got him killed!" Paige wailed. "We got him killed!"

The black waterfall had frozen, completely blocking off their view of the outside. The police car was still halfway inside the house. Nothing remained of the officer, at least nothing that they could see through the windshield.

Adeline knew that her conscience was going to give her many sleepless nights over this. For now, the officer's sacrifice had done one important thing for them: the ghosts seemed as gobsmacked by what had just happened as the humans were.

She made a run for it. Paige did the same thing. They rushed into Naomi's room and pulled the door shut behind them.

"He's dead!" said Paige, sobbing. "I killed him!"

"We'll make it right," Adeline promised, though there didn't seem to be much they could do to counteract a man being dissolved as if submerged in battery acid.

She'd left Boyd behind, and now she'd left Naomi behind, but at the moment Naomi was the safest of them all. As long as the wood she was sitting on didn't rot, she'd be okay.

Paige pressed herself against the door. "It's my fault. I begged him to come help us."

"We didn't know what would happen."

"We knew it might be bad!"

"Honey, it's a horrible thing that happened, but there's nothing we can do about it right now. We have to focus on surviving. We'll work through our grief and our guilt when we're all safe, I promise."

"We're not going to be safe."

"Yes, we are."

"A cop drove his car right through our house and got killed! How the hell are we going to be saved?"

"Watch your language," said Adeline. It was completely a reflexive mother response; she didn't care if Paige cursed right now. An avalanche of profanity, including the f-word and c-word, was totally appropriate.

"Sorry," said Paige.

"I know it seems bad. But we're going to get out of this. All four of us."

"How?"

"I don't know. There has to be a way."

"Why? Why does there have to be a way?"

"Because there just does." Adeline had offered far better arguments in her life, but she wasn't simply trying to fake a sunshiny outlook. She genuinely believed that there was a way out of this. She had no fucking clue what it was, but there was a solution to their problem. There had to be. They couldn't be killed by ghosts in a rotting house. That was ridiculous.

"Is Dad dead?" asked Paige.

Adeline violently shook her head. "No."

"Then where is he?"

"He's in the basement."

"With a ghost?"

"Yes."

"So then he's dead."

"No! Goddamn it, Paige, stop acting like this! Your father is not dead, and we're going to find a way to beat them. Let's make them less scary. Let's give them nicknames."

"What?"

"Nicknames," said Adeline. "The one with the bones? He's Boney now. Only think of him as Boney."

"You've gone insane," said Paige.

"So what? Sanity hasn't worked out for us so far, so why not try something different? Boney. The one who can't breathe—what's his new name?"

"I don't know."

"Think of something. You're creative."

"Chokey?"

"Chokey! Perfect! Boney and Chokey. You can't be afraid of ghosts named Boney and Chokey, right?"

"I guess not."

"What about the last one? The one whose body parts aren't completely attached. What's a good name for him?"

Paige thought for a moment. "Floppy?"

"Floppy works."

"No, Stretchy."

"Stretchy! Boney, Chokey, and Stretchy. The Three Stooges of ghosts. They don't scare me. Do they scare you?"

"I don't know."

"They're jokes. We should be laughing at them. That's what we'll do the next time we see them. Point and laugh."

"Why aren't they trying to get inside?"

"Maybe they got bored and left."

"Maybe they went after Dad."

Adeline let out a sudden sob that she hadn't realized was building up. Paige was right. Boyd was probably dead, and all the goofy nicknames in the world weren't going to save them.

Nobody was going to help them.

"I'll guard the door," said Adeline. "Get a sock or something out of Naomi's drawer. Your eyelid is bleeding again."

CHAPTER TWENTY-ONE

W hat the hell was that?

It sounded like a train had crashed into the house.

That, combined with the thunderous crash from before, made it clear that some serious shit was happening upstairs. Maddox hoped that Fletcher and Heck weren't screwing this up.

"*Hope you've got renter's insurance,*" he told Boyd, jabbing his index finger bone into his back. He was halfway through making the mouth of a smiley face out of bloody holes.

Boyd didn't have a witty response. That was okay. Maddox hadn't said anything witty while his bones were being shattered with a fireplace poker, so he couldn't expect a father of two girls to uphold a higher standard.

Maddox should probably go upstairs to see what was happening. He didn't like the idea of leaving Boyd unattended, but how far could the guy get?

"*I feel like I should check things out up there,*" said Maddox. "*You okay with that? I'd have to slash a couple of tendons to make sure you don't run away.*"

"I'm not going anywhere."

Maddox grinned. *"Yeah, it's true, you're not."*

Honestly, Maddox had nothing against the poor guy. He didn't deserve his fate. Neither did his wife and kids. They seemed like a perfectly decent family. Though they had to die, and die horribly, it was most definitely nothing personal. If Maddox could slaughter a family of assholes, he'd happily take that option, but he had no control over who moved into this house.

He actually didn't know for sure that they had to die horribly. They had to die, yeah, but the "horribly" part was more a feeling than a rule. Nobody had spelled out any rules. This was all instinctual.

Anyway, Boyd wouldn't suffer as much as Maddox had. The pain of that bitch beating him to death had been beyond anything he could have imagined.

And then, shortly after crossing over, he longed for a return to the mild, almost quaint suffering of being beaten to death by a fireplace poker.

Gina had said they weren't going to Hell, but that was a mere technicality. This place could not have been more hellish if Satan were jabbing their asses with a pitchfork while Hitler led the morning exercises. Constant agony. Constant terror. The kind of place where you wanted to just tuck yourself into a corner and go completely insane so that you didn't have to cope with your existence...but insanity would've been too easy. It would've been a cherished gift. A straitjacket and an eternity of mad laughter? Paradise.

It was confusing how things worked. Sometimes it felt like they were in their bodies, sometimes it felt like they were watching themselves. The flow of time was irrelevant; Maddox had no idea if they'd been gone for days, weeks, years, decades, or what, though it wasn't like the family had android servants or a teleportation machine, so maybe it hadn't been that long. The place that wasn't officially Hell was like a nightmare where everything happened in flashes, and things would fade from your memory shortly after they happened, but you'd keep waking up into something worse. It was like being in a horror flick where the hero would wake up and say "Oh, thank goodness, it was only a dream!" and then the monster would drop onto his bed because he was *still* in the dream, ha ha, fooled the audience, repeated an infinite number of times.

It all kind of sounded like how you'd perceive the world when you were insane, but Maddox was always completely aware of what was happening to him in the moment. He always knew that his hellish existence was the result what Gina had done to him. He would not eventually wake up in his own bed and breathe a sigh of relief.

But then—and he had no idea how long it took for this to happen—he could see the real world again. Just the house where he'd died. He wasn't sure *how* he could see it; it wasn't as if they were floating outside the house, or gazing through a magical mirror, or seeing images projected onto a flayed body, but they could see it. All three of them.

And they knew they could get back.

They could steal energy. Drain *life*, though that sounded corny.

None of them really understood how it worked. Maybe the power of love or some shit radiated some kind of force that they could feed upon. The draining did weird stuff. Made the family sick. Rotted their food. Made the older girl succumb to some darkness she'd kept in the back of her developing brain. Made her think a contact lens was crushing her eye, even though it had fallen out and stuck to the side of the toilet. Made the younger girl want to swim with the fishes.

Finally, when Maddox, Heck, and Fletcher had drained enough, the family snapped back to normal. Things would've been looking up for them, but, alas, suddenly they had three otherworldly home invaders.

And now was the fun part.

Oh, things remained awful. The three of them were still in constant agony (at least he was, and there was no reason to believe it was different for his partners) but that had been the status quo for a long time, and it was something you eventually got used to, more or less. And it was hard to control this new ghost-version of himself, but he was getting the hang of it quickly. When they first materialized, he'd been worried that it might be like some kind of stroke-recovery-victim thing where he'd spend months or years learning to walk again, so this wasn't bad at all.

It was almost over. One dead husband, one dead wife, two dead little girls, and then he'd be back to normal.

At least that's what he believed would happen. The first phase of the plan had worked as expected, so presumably his instincts were correct on the second part as well. Heck and Fletcher hadn't come downstairs to report that the family had escaped, so Maddox assumed that the barrier was working properly. Nobody could escape the house. Nobody could get in the house. And there was no ticking clock. They had as long as they needed to kill the Gardner family. Boyd and his loved ones could hide away, sleep in shifts, and survive on whatever food in the house wasn't rotten, but they'd eventually die.

Maddox didn't share this with Boyd. He didn't want the poor guy to lose all hope. It wouldn't be as enjoyable to torture him to death if he succumbed to nihilistic despair.

"*Hey.*"

Maddox looked up. Heck stood at the top of the staircase.

"*What's wrong?*"

"*Nothing's wrong. It's actually pretty fuckin' great up here. You should come up and see it.*"

"*See what?*"

"*It's better if you see for yourself.*"

"*Give me a hint.*"

"*Dead cop.*"

Maddox grinned. "*Oh, yeah, I do wanna see that.*"

"*It's crazy what happened. You won't even believe it.*"

"*You kill any of his family?*"

"*Nah. Not yet.*"

Maddox patted Boyd on the shoulder. "*You hear that? You still have something to live for. I bet that makes you feel all warm and fuzzy inside. Go ahead and say something defiant if you want. I won't get mad.*"

"Fuck you."

"*So was that your defiant statement? Or was that in reference to me telling you to go ahead and say something defiant?*"

"*C'mon, Maddox,*" said Heck. "*We don't have time for this shit.*"

"*Not true. We have all the time in the world.*"

"*Well, I personally would like to end the agony as soon as possible.*"

"*You're right, you're right, fair enough.*" Maddox held up his index finger. He wished it wouldn't keep healing itself. He braced himself for the pain, and then the bone tore through his transparent skin. It hurt every bit as much as he assumed it would if his body was still flesh and blood.

"*What are you doing?*" asked Heck.

"*Going to slice his Achilles tendons. Keep him from going anywhere.*"

"*What if he bleeds to death while you're gone?*"

"*Is that against the rules?*"

"*Doesn't seem like a horrible enough way to go.*"

"*Hmm.*"

"*Just break his leg.*"

"*How?*"

"*I don't know,*" said Heck. "*Push him down the stairs. You know what, just forget it. You can see it later.*"

"*No, no, I don't want to miss out. He's not going to spoil anything if he crawls a couple of feet. Let's go.*"

Maddox walked upstairs, leaving poor little bleeding Boyd behind. Truthfully, the guy was in bad enough shape that he might bleed to death without his heels being slashed open, but Maddox wouldn't be gone long.

As soon as they stepped into the kitchen, he saw all of the rubble on the living room floor. The whole ceiling had come down! Holy shit!

"*How'd that happen?*"

"*Fletcher rotted it out from under them.*"

"*We can do that?*"

"*Apparently.*"

"*Good to know. Where's the cop?*"

Maddox followed Heck into the living room. He'd seen many surreal, grisly sights on the other side, but he couldn't remember any of them. He was very confident that he'd never seen a police car imbedded halfway through a living room wall.

He went over and peered through the windshield. *"Where's the dead cop?"*

"He should be right..." Heck peered into the car as well. *"Shit, I guess he completely dissolved. You can see a piece of his uniform on the seat. You should've seen him melt. It was gruesome as hell."*

"Oh well." Maddox looked over at Fletcher. *"Why are you just standing there?"*

"Babysitting."

"What?"

Fletcher casually pointed up. The younger girl, Naomi, was still up in what used to be the attic. She didn't seem to be in any danger of falling, but she was crying and she sure looked scared.

Maddox waved to her.

"You can't reach her?" he asked.

"Not quite."

"Why don't you rot the wood and make her fall?" he asked.

Fletcher tried to answer, but couldn't get a coherent sentence out through his choking.

"We can't reach it," said Heck. *"We rotted the wall but it's not going up high enough."*

"Throw some shit at her."

"When we're able to pick stuff up, we'll get right on that."

"Where's the mom and other kid?"

Heck pointed to a closed door. *"Hiding in there."*

"Get in there and kill them."

"We are. Just thought you'd want to see the melted cop, that's all."

"And now I have. I'm heading back downstairs."

Maddox returned to the kitchen. He paused to glance at the refrigerator. That's what he missed more than anything else: food. Well, food and the lack of endless excruciating pain. The first thing he was going to do when he was back in a regular body was get the biggest, juiciest, Ribeye steak he could find, slathered in A-1 sauce, with a loaded baked potato and a cold beer.

He walked down the steps. Boyd had crawled away from the staircase but he hadn't gotten very far. Maddox couldn't be mad at him. Actually, he would've been kind of disgusted with Boyd if the guy was exactly where he'd left him.

"*Accomplish anything while I was gone?*" Maddox asked.

Boyd didn't respond.

"*Let's pick up where we left off.*"

CHAPTER TWENTY-TWO

"M om...?"

Adeline looked up. Paige handed her one of Naomi's shirts. Adeline thanked her and used it to wipe her eyes. She wished she could stop crying, but under the circumstances, she thought she was setting a good example for her daughter simply by not dropping to the floor and shrieking at the top of her lungs. Or going catatonic.

She knew Naomi was safe for now, because she hadn't alerted them with a scream. She had no idea if Boyd was alive or dead. She wanted to believe that deep in her heart she knew her husband was still alive, but that was fairy tale bullshit. It didn't matter how she felt in her heart; if the ghosts hadn't murdered him yet, he was still alive. If they had, he was lying dead in the cold basement. Her feelings had nothing to do with it.

Why weren't the ghosts trying to get into Naomi's bedroom?

The doorknob began to jiggle.

"Boyd?" she asked, even though Adeline knew it wasn't him. Boyd would have announced himself before trying to open the door.

"*Yes, it's me.*" For a moment Adeline thought the ghost was trying to fool her with a terrible impression of Boyd's voice. Then she realized that the ghost was just mocking her.

Adeline gestured for Paige to get into position. Their plan wasn't complex. It was, in fact, absurdly simple: let the ghost (or hopefully more than one) come into Naomi's room after them, get past it, and barricade it in there. Same plan that didn't work in the basement. This would be more effective, long-term, if the ghost didn't damage the door, so they'd left it unlocked.

Paige climbed underneath Naomi's bed.

The doorknob continued to jiggle. Apparently the ghost couldn't get a solid enough grip to turn it.

Then the door swung open. Adeline stepped backwards, staying behind it.

The dismembered ghost—Stretchy—walked into the room.

Paige, as planned, jostled the blanket a bit, giving away her location.

The ghost moved toward the bed.

As it crossed the room, Adeline came out from behind the door. "I'm right here, you blind piece of shit!"

The ghost turned to look at her. Paige rolled out from under the bed, jumped to her feet, and raced for the door. The red goo stretched out as the ghost tried to grab her, but she dodged its hand and made it out of Naomi's room, followed immediately by Adeline, who pulled the door shut.

They both ran for the couch and pushed it across the living room. Chokey stepped in front of the couch to block it, but it passed right through him, slamming into the bedroom door.

"Jump!" Adeline shouted. "Jump now!"

If Naomi hesitated, the choking ghost might get her. She didn't hesitate. She leapt from her perch. The couch wasn't directly underneath it, but it was close enough that she wouldn't have to make a more dramatic leap than she did in any given gymnastics class.

As she fell through the air, there was a split-second where Adeline thought she wasn't going to make it. She'd hit the floor and break her legs. Adeline had this sudden weird, inexplicable image of Naomi striking the wood and her legs shattering like glass, all the way to her torso, sharp red pieces flying everywhere.

Instead, she landed on the couch, bounced off the cushion, and then hit the floor. It looked like it hurt, but she got right up and took Adeline's hand as the three of them ran out of the living room.

If Chokey weren't there, they could've moved more furniture and done a much better job of trapping his friend in Naomi's bedroom. They'd have to hope that the couch kept him stuck in there for a while.

They stopped outside of Boyd and Adeline's bedroom. She desperately wanted to rush down into the basement to help Boyd (if he could still be helped) (*stop thinking that way*) but if she could manage to trap Chokey in a different room and then move every piece of furniture in the house in front of those two doors, they'd only have Boney to contend with.

The nicknames weren't helping.

The choking ghost looked back and forth between them and Naomi's bedroom door, as if unsure whether it should try to move the couch or go after its prey. Adeline had done the "Come and get me!" trick too many times; it was unlikely to fool the ghost again. Their best bet was

211

to go into the bedroom as if hoping not to be pursued.

Adeline, Paige, and Naomi went into the bedroom but didn't close the door yet. This was going to be more difficult with three of them, but they might be able to rework the same plan. Lure him in, get past him, then block the door. Nice and simple.

"You're both going to hide under the bed," Adeline whispered. "When he gets the door open, Paige, you move the blanket like you did before so he knows you're under there. When you hear me talk to him, both of you get out from under the bed and run out the door as fast as you can."

Paige and Naomi nodded.

Adeline peeked out into the hallway.

Crap. The choking ghost was trying to push the couch away.

Back to the other tactic. "Hey!" Adeline shouted. "Over here!"

The ghost ignored her.

"New plan," Adeline told the girls. "I'm going to get your father. Keep checking on the ghost. If he comes after you, lock the door and drag everything you can in front of it."

"Bring him back safe," said Paige.

"I will." She gave them a brief hug then left the room. She walked quickly but quietly, hoping that the choking ghost would be focused on the couch and not see her departure.

She promised herself that she'd keep it together if Boyd was dead. She'd immediately return to her daughters to protect them. There'd be plenty of time for sorrow, second-guessing, and self-loathing later.

- - -

"*Almost done with the smiley face,*" said the bruised ghost, jabbing his finger-bone into Boyd's back once again. "*Well, the mouth anyway. Just looks like a U. But I promise, it's gonna be a fine piece of art.*"

Boyd wasn't sure exactly how many holes the ghost had poked into his back—at least a dozen—but he wished he could get used to the pain, or at least go numb. Each time the ghost punctured his skin, it hurt as much as the previous time.

"*Does it bother you to be so helpless?*"

"Yes," said Boyd. Why lie?

"*Do you wish I'd put you out of your misery?*"

"No."

"*You sure?*"

"Are you asking for real or are you just taunting me?"

Maddox chuckled. "*Mostly taunting you. I'm not really sure I need to keep dragging this out, though. I hate to leave the smiley face unfinished, but I feel like I've caused you enough torment to pretty much complete your role in the ritual. I say 'pretty much' because you still have to die, of course.*"

"Of course."

"*I can't promise that it'll be quick and easy. I could jab a bone through your eyeball and into your brain, but I think I'm leaning more toward very slowly slashing your throat. Not too drawn out, but sufficiently horrible.*"

Boyd didn't know what to say. He couldn't fight back. Couldn't run. He certainly didn't want to amuse the asshole by begging for his life.

There was absolutely nothing he could do.

Except...pretend that he didn't see Adeline at the top of the stairs.

She was holding a fire extinguisher. Though Boyd didn't know what she intended to do with it, he was confident that she'd worked out an awesome plan.

Boyd had let out many winces of pain since the torture process began, but his next wince was the loudest one yet, on purpose. "Enough!" he said. "I can't take this shit any more! Just kill me, for God's sake! Just jam it into the back of my neck and be done with it!"

"Didn't we just finish discussing this?"

"It's not going to work, you know."

"What's not?"

"The ritual."

"You don't know anything about the ritual besides what I've told you. What are you trying to do, distract—?"

It would've been far too much to hope for that Adeline could've actually snuck all the way down the stairs without Maddox noticing. In fact, she didn't even make it down the first step. But once he glanced up at her, Adeline ran down the stairs and let loose with the fire extinguisher, blasting both of them.

Boyd didn't know if it had an impact on the ghost. It would be delightful to think that the ghosts disintegrated upon being sprayed, but it was unlikely that there was any kind of physical effect. It was a pretty good distraction, though.

Time to summon that burst of strength.

Boyd crawled up the stairs as quickly as he could. It hurt like hell to move that rapidly, but this pain was a lot more bearable than spending more time in the basement with Maddox. Adeline kept blasting the ghost with the extinguisher. Presumably she couldn't blind something that didn't have corporeal eyes, meaning that Maddox wouldn't claw at his face screaming, *"You've blinded me!*

You bitch, you've blinded me!" But if she could confuse and disorient him for a few seconds, that might be enough.

Boyd smashed his already-bleeding chin against one of the steps. He knew he was in very, very bad shape when he accidentally hit his face while crawling up stairs.

The whoosh of the fire extinguisher turned to a sputter. Was it really empty already? Hadn't Jack checked that?

Adeline flung the extinguisher at Maddox. Boyd didn't look back, but he assumed that it passed harmlessly through the ghost. Adeline grabbed Boyd's hands and helped him race up the stairs, then slammed the door.

Boyd wanted to give her a hug. That wasn't part of her plan. She sprinted to their bedroom door and knocked. "It's us! Let us in!"

The dismembered ghost stood in the living room, looking like it was unsuccessfully trying to pull a couch. Had the entire ceiling collapsed? Boyd had thought it had been a rather eventful day for him personally, but apparently he'd missed out on some stuff.

The bedroom door opened.

Adeline and Boyd rushed inside and pulled the door closed.

"Push everything you can in front of the door!" said Adeline. "Here, we'll start with the bed." Adeline, Paige, and Naomi began to scoot the bed across the room, while Boyd braced himself against the wall to keep from passing out.

He was covered in his own blood, but he didn't think he was going to die.

At least, not soon.

Of course, there was no reason to believe that they'd be free anytime soon.

- - -

Once the bed was in place, and a dresser was stacked on top of it, there was time for hugs. Simulated hugs, anyway—Boyd was too torn up to want his loved ones to actually squeeze him. One of Naomi's standard hugs might have legitimately killed him.

"So do we have a plan of action beyond this?" he asked.

Adeline shook her head. "No. I'd like to say that we can just wait for help, but..."

"We murdered a police officer," said Paige.

"What?"

"That's not what she means," said Adeline. "But a police officer died trying to rescue us."

"How?"

Adeline shared a tale of cars crashing through walls and corrosive ooze eating away members of law enforcement. Boyd felt sick to his stomach, both because an innocent man had died and because this seemed to mean there was no way out. The house was completely sealed.

"People outside have to be able to do something, don't they?" he asked. "I mean, what would happen if they took a great big wrecking ball and knocked off the roof? Would that gunk seal the whole thing up?"

"No idea," said Adeline. "I think the ghosts will find a way in here before somebody decides to knock off the roof. My big concern is that somebody outside could try something a little less drastic and have the same thing happen to them that happened to the cop."

Boyd sighed. He hadn't even considered that more

innocent people could die trying to save them. Hopefully the circumstances of the cop's death were bizarre enough to keep anybody from coming too close.

"So we just wait?" asked Boyd.

"I'm not going to wait," said Paige. "I'm going to break a hole through the wall. Maybe they all don't work the same way. I won't put my hand through it or anything."

"It's too dangerous," said Adeline.

"It didn't squirt out at him. It poured straight down. If I'm careful and know what to expect, I'll be fine."

"You just said that maybe they don't all work the same way."

Paige frowned. "All right. But I don't want to sit around until they get us."

"I don't either," said Adeline. "We'll figure something out. For now, let's get your father patched up."

Fortunately, their bathroom was connected to the bedroom. It wasn't a fully stocked pharmacy, but there were plenty of bandages to go around. Boyd did not scream when the antiseptic was applied to his wounds. He did shed a few tears, and felt no shame about his daughters seeing him cry.

"Do you hear that?" asked Adeline.

"Hear what?"

She looked up. "Sounds like a helicopter."

"*Attention,*" said a megaphone-amplified voice from outside. "*This is the police. Come out of the residence with your hands in the air. I repeat, come out of the residence with your hands in the air.*"

"So," said Adeline. "Did things just get better for us, or a lot worse?"

217

- - -

Gina Atherton was enjoying a hot cup of decaffeinated coffee as she watched *Parks and Recreation* on television. Binge watching, her nephew Danny had said it was called. She'd never been much of a TV viewer, but being able to choose whatever show she wanted to see, instead of being at the mercy of the programming schedule, and being able to watch all of the episodes in order from the beginning made her truly appreciate the almost magical innovations in technology. Granted, it meant that she was on her sofa watching her sixth hour of TV instead of going out and doing things, but she'd never been a terribly social person anyway.

When her phone rang, she almost ignored it, but a picture of Jack Ponter appeared on the screen. (Being able to see a picture of whoever was calling her was a wonderful thing. She had no idea how Danny set that up.) She didn't feel like talking to Jack, but he probably needed approval on something for the rental house, and she wasn't going to shirk her duties.

"Hello, Jack," she said, answering it. She wondered if he was surprised that she knew it was him. Most likely not; he was younger than her and probably knew all about the things you could do with cellular telephones.

"Hi, Gina. Sorry to bother you."

"It's no problem at all. How can I help you?"

"I don't think there's anything either of us can do about it, but police have surrounded the house you rented to the Gardner family..."

CHAPTER TWENTY-THREE

When Gina arrived ten minutes later, Jack, along with numerous reporters and various onlookers, was already standing just outside of a barricade that the police had set up outside of the house. Inside the barricade were at least six police cars and a fire truck. A helicopter circled overhead.

"What on earth is happening in there?" she asked him. "Why does the house look like that?"

"I have no idea," Jack admitted. "They can't get in there. Nobody inside is answering. Apparently a cop died—look, you can see the back half of his car."

Gina narrowed her eyes. A police car was indeed imbedded in the front of her house, but what caught her attention was the black substance that filled in the gaps. It was as if somebody had used tar to repair the hole but forgotten to remove the automobile first.

She didn't know what it was, but it was not natural. And if something unnatural was happening in the house...well, her night of bloody vengeance over a year ago might have come back to haunt her.

Gina ducked underneath the yellow police tape.

"Whoa, whoa, where are you going?" asked Jack.

"It's my house."

"That doesn't mean you can just walk through the barricade! It might not be safe!"

Gina ignored him and kept walking. An officer immediately accosted her. "Stay behind the tape, please, ma'am."

"It's my house."

"Come with me, please."

The officer led her to a gray-haired, tired-looking man with a megaphone. Gina doubted that the cup of coffee he was drinking was decaf.

"This woman says it's her house," said the officer.

The man nodded, gulped down some of his coffee, and looked at Gina. "So maybe you can tell me what the hell is happening in there?"

"Unfortunately, I can't. But I'd like to go inside and find out."

"We can't get inside. A neighbor says that one of my men tried to shoot through a window and it sealed back up. The people in there aren't talking any more, but apparently they said not to touch the door. Until we find out what that stuff is around the car, we're not taking any chances."

"I'll take the chance." Gina headed for the house.

"Hey!" The man grabbed her by the arm. "You're not going in there."

"Are you really going to physically restrain an old woman?" Gina tugged her arm away from him. "Are you going to shoot me in the back?"

"You're not that old."

"Thank you."

"But I can't let you go in there."

"I'm not asking you to give me your blessing. I'd just

like you not to tackle me or shoot me." Gina resumed walking toward the house. She felt confident that they would not open fire on her, though if somebody chose to drag her away, there was only so much resistance she could put up.

She made it all the way to the front door.

"*Hold up, everyone,*" said the man into the megaphone. Gina assumed he was the police chief, but she wasn't an expert on who got to hold the megaphone. "Ma'am, please be careful."

Gina opened the front door.

What the hell had they done to her property? It looked terrible from the outside, but she hadn't expected the entire living room ceiling to have crashed to the floor! This was going to cost a fortune to repair! Goddamned tenants.

Now she was just trying to fool herself into thinking that this damage was caused by excessive partying, instead of something sinister. She closed the door behind her. If things inside this house were as bad as she suspected, she might not want witnesses.

"Hello?" she called out.

Somebody answered with a choking noise.

It was the tall bald one. Cliff Fletcher. The one she'd forced to drown himself in the koi pond. She didn't know if he was a ghost or an astral projection or what, but she could see right through him.

This was unexpected.

As she stared at him, he filled in a bit. Became slightly less transparent. She could still see through him, but not quite as clearly as a few seconds ago.

He seemed to notice this as well. He held his hand up in front of his face, then reached down with both hands and pulled a couch out away from the door of what had been her guest room.

The door swung open. Hector Clarke, the thin man whose arms, legs, and head she'd chopped off, emerged. *"Hey, did things suddenly get easier for you, too?"* he asked.

Cliff pointed at Gina. Hector broke into a huge grin.

"It's her! Oh my God, it's her! I can't believe it! Hey, bitch, I think your presence just made us stronger!"

Gina decided that it was time for her to leave now. She'd assumed that the gentlemen she'd so brutally murdered were responsible for what was happening to the house, but she hadn't expected to actually *see* them.

She turned around, grabbed the doorknob, and yelped at a sensation that was like getting stung by twenty wasps at once. It left a thick, black burn mark on her palm.

She wasn't trapped in here, was she? She couldn't be.

Okay, just because the doorknob hurt to turn didn't mean it wouldn't turn at all. She picked up a wad of pink insulation and used it to protect her hand as she grabbed the doorknob again.

It didn't work. It hurt every bit as much this time, and though she forced herself to withstand the pain for several seconds, the doorknob would not budge.

She should not have closed the door behind her.

"Nobody gets out," said Hector. *"Not even you, apparently."*

"Is somebody inside the house?" a woman's voice called out. It sounded like she was behind a closed door in the hallway. Gina had never spoken to her, but presumably this was Adeline Gardner. Gina hoped so; she didn't want any more participants in this nightmare.

Gina wasn't much of a runner. This was a good time to start.

She ran. The murderers followed.

"It's Gina Atherton!" she shouted. "I'm the owner! Let me in!"

She could hear the sound of furniture being moved. But not nearly quickly enough. She ran into the room next to it instead, slamming the door and locking it. Thank God that doorknob hadn't behaved like the other one. Apparently only doors leading to the outside were supernaturally booby-trapped.

"Don't open the door!" she shouted. "They were right behind me!"

"Can you help us?" Adeline asked.

Gina didn't have a good answer for that. She supposed that she was more valuable than some random person off the street, but she wasn't some amazing spellcaster who used witchcraft on a daily basis. Her sister had been the expert. Gina had never imagined that these three men would return, and she couldn't just snap her fingers and send them back.

"Maybe," she said.

There was a black spot on the wall next to the door that she hadn't noticed before. No, wait, now there were two. And they were getting bigger.

"They're rotting our wall!" said Adeline.

Ah, so that's what was happening. Wonderful.

If she'd known that she was going to get trapped inside the house with the three men she'd killed, Gina would have taken the time to formulate a plan before walking through the front door. She had some ideas on how to proceed, but they were all *extremely* flawed.

"Mine, too," said Gina. She wished she could speak privately with the family instead of having to be loud enough to be heard through the wall. "I'll meet you in the basement."

She didn't want to leave the relative safety of the bedroom this soon, but at least she'd sort of have the element of surprise if she left now instead of waiting for the wall to fall apart. She opened the door and ran out into the hallway. Hector tried to grab her but missed. He tried again, and this time his arm stretched out. Well, no, his arm stayed the same length, but whatever that red crap was that held his body parts to his torso stretched.

By chopping him to pieces, Gina had basically given him super ghost powers. What a treat.

The other bedroom door opened. The Gardners emerged, and they looked like they'd gone through a war. The father, Boyd, looked particularly bad, but the older girl might have lost an eye. This wasn't Gina's fault. There was no way she could have known. She'd banished three psycho killers from the earth. Thirst for vengeance aside, she was trying to save their future victims. She refused to accept the blame for what was happening here.

Hector was blocking her path to the living room, but luckily Gina wasn't trying to go in that direction. Much more problematic: Fletcher, who'd apparently been the one rotting the wall to the other bedroom, was blocking the path to the basement.

Even more problematic: their leader, Maddox, who looked as hideous in ghost form as he did when she'd buried him, was also in the hallway, standing behind Fletcher.

One ghost to the left, two ghosts to the right...

"*Well, well, well,*" said Maddox. "*I didn't think we'd see you here. I thought we'd have to break into your home at night.*"

The ghosts were closing in.

"Can they physically hurt us?" Gina asked Boyd. He was covered in blood, so it had been a silly question.

The most obvious course of action was to go right the hell back into the bedrooms, but if the ghosts could get through the wall, that was far too temporary of a solution.

Gina had no power over these men.

But did they know that?

"Stop!" she shouted at them, holding up her hand. "Come one step closer and I will send you back!"

All three of the ghosts stopped.

"You may have found a way to escape your torment, but I'll return you there if you don't cooperate! Is that what you want? Do you want more hellish torture, or do you want to get the fuck out of our way?"

"*Why are you here?*" asked Maddox.

"I'm here to work out an arrangement with these nice people. They aren't part of this."

"*Yes, they are. An important part.*"

Gina shook her head. "You've got it wrong. You're trying to return to physical bodies, right?"

"*That's right.*"

"You don't need them. There's another way."

"*Which is...?*"

"Which is to get the fuck out of our way, like I said." Gina considered waving her hand in the air, as if she was about to cast a spell, but decided that would be overselling it.

"*Okay,*" said Maddox, moving aside.

Hector didn't move.

"*Heck, do what she said.*"

Hector reluctantly stepped against the wall, giving them enough room to pass. Gina, Boyd, Adeline, Paige, and Naomi slowly walked through the hallway into the kitchen.

"*What's next?*" Maddox asked.

"Next you let us go downstairs undisturbed. I don't want to see your hideous face while I'm talking to these people. Do you understand?"

"*How do I know you aren't trying to trick us?*"

"You don't. You accept that giving me a few minutes to talk things out with your innocent victims is better than me immediately banishing you again. And the more you talk, the less charitable I'm feeling."

Maddox looked unconvinced, but he didn't try to stop Gina as she led the Gardners down the stairs into the basement. They walked slowly, both to give the impression that they weren't trying to make a hasty escape, and because Boyd looked like he could barely move.

Gina flipped the light switch. Nothing happened.

"The bulb shattered," said Adeline.

"So we'll chat in the dark." She closed the door as they walked down the stairs.

"Can you really send them back?" Paige whispered.

"No. I would've done it right there. And they're going to figure that out soon, even though all three of them are idiots. So we don't have a lot of time."

"You can't send them back, but can you stop them?" Boyd asked.

Gina hesitated.

"You can't stop them?"

"I didn't come in here wearing a white hat and pretending to be your savior," said Gina. "I can at least say that you're better off now than you were before I got here. That's something, right?"

"I guess. Is there something you can actually do to help us?"

"There might be."

"What?"

"You're not going to like my answer."

CHAPTER TWENTY-FOUR

"W hat's your answer?" asked Boyd.

"First of all, this is all confidential," said Gina. "You don't speak a word of what I'm about to tell you to anybody else, okay?"

"Because it'll sound crazy?"

"That's part of it, I guess. Mostly it's because I murdered your home invaders. Don't talk to the cops about it. If I help get you out of this, you tell them that we didn't speak to each other. You didn't even know I was in the house. Got it?"

"Got it," said Boyd. He'd suspected the whole "murdered them before they became ghosts" part anyway.

"I puppeteered them. Put my own thoughts into their minds, made them think they should come to my house, this house, to apologize. I drowned one of them in the koi pond, I chopped up another one with an axe right around where we're standing right now, and I beat the last one to death with a fireplace poker, also right around where we're standing now. It wasn't in cold blood. They did far worse to my sister."

"Why did they kill your sister?" asked Naomi.

"They were hired by somebody who needed to kill a witch."

"Why did they need to kill a witch?"

"For a really awful ritual that would have given him her power. Don't worry, I ruined his plan. Our concern right now is getting rid of the ghosts."

"Right," said Boyd. "I'm still waiting on the answer I'm not going to like."

"If their three corpses were lying on the floor in front of us, it would be perfect. I'd send them back and they'd be out of your hair. The problem is that I only buried one of them in the yard. The other two are buried hundreds of miles away. I thought that by keeping their bodies apart, they'd be trapped alone on the other side, but obviously I got that part wrong."

"So we need to figure out a way to bring the other bodies here?" Adeline asked.

"No. I mean, yes, in theory that would work, but even if I could get the message out to somebody who was willing to do it, it would take a few hours, not counting the time to dig them up. I can't even get Cliff's body. If I could get out of here, it's not like the police would just stand around and watch me dig up a corpse."

"Which one is Cliff?"

"The tall bald one. Cliff Fletcher."

"The choking one."

"Right. I buried him in my flower garden. Which means that his body is..." Gina turned and pointed. "...on the other side of that wall."

"Then all we need to do is break through a concrete basement wall," said Adeline. "No problem. Oh, I guess we also have to worry about the black ooze that melted the cop. No biggie."

"Your sarcasm is setting a bad example for your daughters. I'm not saying that we can get to his body. I'm saying that maybe, *maybe*, no guarantees, if we can lure Mr. Fletcher down here and get him *reasonably* close to where he's buried, I might be able to send his ghost back to his body."

"So he'd be buried alive?" asked Boyd.

"Yes."

"I actually like that answer."

"Being buried alive is better than what he was going through on the other side, but, yes, he would cease to be a problem for us. That still leaves the other two."

"Right."

"Have you been able to fight back?" Gina asked. "I'm sure I know what you're going to say but I want to make sure I have accurate information."

"No," said Boyd. "They can hurt us but we can't hurt them."

"But you might be able to fight them on equal ground."

"Meaning...?"

"I've never done this before. Never tried to do this before. Never even considered doing this before. I don't know if it will work. I don't know if it's the right thing to do even if it does work. It could cause things to be infinitely worse than they are."

This lady had more disclaimers than an antidepressant commercial. "Please just tell me what you're thinking," said Boyd.

"I can send one of you to the other side."

"To Hell?"

"To the place that's not quite Hell, yes."

She was absolutely right. Boyd did not like this answer.

"The benefit is that I can actually fight them?"

Gina nodded. "If it works, and if you can withstand the agony and terror, and if you can find them, I think you might be able to fight them."

"Aren't they in the house, though?"

"They're not *entirely* in the house."

"I don't understand."

"I don't, either. That's why I keep making excuses."

"Let's pretend it does work," said Boyd. "Best case scenario, if you take Cliff Fletcher out of the equation, it's still a two-against-one battle, right?"

"Yes. But you have an advantage. Wisdom that I'm going to share with you. When you cross over, treat it like a sick joke. Have fun with it. And that may give you the power to control it."

"That sounds really messed up."

Gina nodded. "It is."

"Can you pull me back out?"

"I believe so."

"'I believe so' is pretty weak."

"I agree," said Gina.

"Okay, so, to recap: I can risk being stuck in Hell forever, or we can sit around and wait for the ghosts to kill us?"

"That's how I see it. You've been trapped in the house longer than me, so you might have a different perspective."

Boyd shook his head. "Sounds about right to me." If he thought about it too much, the unimaginable horror of this scheme would make him decide that "wait for the ghosts to kill us" was the right way to go, so he decided not to think about it. "Let's do it."

"Boyd, no!" said Adeline.

"We don't have a choice," Boyd insisted. "I can beat these jokers in a fair fight."

"It wouldn't be a fair fight!"

"I can beat them, I promise." Of course Adeline knew that he could promise no such thing; this was more for Paige and Naomi's benefit.

"If somebody has to go, it needs to be me," said Adeline. "You're too badly hurt."

"His injuries won't matter on the other side," said Gina.

"See?" said Boyd. "It'll be worth it if only to stop bleeding to death."

"Your body here will continue to bleed," said Gina.

Boyd didn't want to talk to her anymore. He pulled Paige and Naomi close, though not close enough to aggravate his many wounds. "I have to do this," he said. "I'll be thinking about you and Mom the whole time, and it'll keep me safe. Nothing is going to happen to me."

He knew that his daughters were going to beg him not to do this, but what choice did he have? If he had to sacrifice himself to save his family, he wouldn't hesitate. Not even if he was condemning himself to an eternity of suffering. Though, again, it was a decision he wanted to finalize quickly, before he started weighing the pros and cons.

"What do you have to do?" Boyd asked. "You don't have to actually kill my body, right?"

"I'm sending you to a very bad place," said Gina. "It requires death or blood."

"Death *or* blood, not death *and* blood, right?"

"Yes."

"Well, I've got the blood part covered."

"Previously spilled blood won't work."

233

"Of course it won't."

"Don't go, Daddy," said Naomi, burying her face into his chest. It hurt, but he didn't stop her.

"I'm going to be totally fine," Boyd assured her. She was eight years old. Too old to believe in Santa Claus, and thus too old to believe that her father would be totally fine if a witch sent him to Hell.

"Children, step away," said Gina. She said it softly, but there was a frightening edge to her voice that caused Paige and Naomi to step away from Boyd without hesitation. "Boyd, give me your arm."

"What are you going to do to it?" Boyd asked. He suddenly worried that the answer was "chop it off."

"Draw fresh blood." She grabbed his arm with both hands, then gave it a violent twist, wringing blood out of the long cut Maddox had given him. It was not the worst pain he'd experienced today, eliciting a really loud wince instead of a scream, but it was certainly unpleasant. Gina continued doing this for at least thirty seconds. Boyd's eyes had not adjusted to the darkness well enough to gauge the size of the pool of blood on the floor. He could, however, see that the gash was now about an inch longer on each end.

He could hear Adeline, Paige, and Naomi all weeping.

Gina stopped twisting.

"Are we done?" Boyd asked through gritted teeth.

"We're done with *that* part."

The upstairs door opened. All three ghosts were there. They were bound to realize they'd been conned eventually, but Boyd hoped they hadn't come to that realization quite yet.

"*Finished with your chat?*" asked Maddox.

"Almost," said Gina. She ran her fingers along Boyd's

wound, using both hands.

"*We're done waiting.*"

Gina curled her fingers. Oh, shit, she wasn't really going to...

She dug her fingers into the gash.

The ghosts began to walk down the stairs. Maddox was in front, and his ribcage burst from his chest again.

Gina pulled her fingers apart, prying open the wound. *This* was the worst pain Boyd had experienced today.

And then he wasn't in the basement anymore.

He didn't know where he was. A desert? Why would he be in a desert?

No, he was on an iceberg.

In a jungle?

A womb?

All of these places at once? None of them? Was he still in the basement and just hallucinating?

One thing he did know: the pain of Gina prying open the wound on his arm had already been demoted to second place.

He screamed until his jaw exploded, spraying flesh, bone and blood an infinite distance.

CHAPTER TWENTY-FIVE

*B*oyd dropped to the floor.

Adeline prayed he was just unconscious. She crouched down next to him and grabbed his wrist, which was slick with blood, trying to find a pulse.

"Stop!" Gina shouted.

For an instant Adeline thought she was talking to her. Then she realized that Gina was, of course, talking to the ghosts.

"*What did you do to him?*" the bruised ghost asked.

"He's at peace now. You won't be able to drag him back with you."

The ghost sneered. "*I feel like you don't quite understand our intentions.*"

"Leave this house," said Gina. "Immediately."

"*If we could leave, we'd be long gone from this shithole.*" The ghost pointed to Paige and Naomi. "*You made those kids orphans for no reason. That's all on you.*"

"I accept the responsibility."

"*You're trembling a bit, old lady. Sure you're not trying to bullshit us? If you could really twitch your nose and send us back to Hell, why do you look so scared?*"

"That's a ridiculous question and you know it."

"*Is it? Because I feel like I could throw you onto the floor and rape you to death.*" The ghost ran his hand over the protruding broken rib bones. "*Lots of bones inside of you all at once. They'll all hurt, but some more than others.*"

"You've crossed to the other side, seen evidence of life after death, gained knowledge that has been sought by humanity since the beginning of man's creation, and the best you can do is make dick jokes?"

The ghost stepped closer. The other two ghosts did the same.

"*It's cute that you think it was a joke. If it were a joke, there would've been an amusing punchline. I meant in a completely serious way that I would literally throw you to the basement floor and rape you while the broken bones of my ribcage penetrate your chest, in and out, in and out. That seems to me like a pretty unpleasant way to go. Not as bad as what we did to your sister, but...*"

Adeline couldn't imagine the trauma that hearing this was inflicting upon Paige and Naomi, but that was a concern for later. For now, she still couldn't locate a pulse on Boyd's wrist or his neck, and she didn't think he was breathing.

"Say what you want about me," said Gina. "Don't disrespect my sister."

"*Oh, we already disrespected her to death. Do you even know everything that happened to her, or did you only see the end result? I can give you a blow by blow if you want.*"

"You're playing with fire."

"*No, we're playing with a sad, pathetic old hag who would have done something to us by now if she could. One warning was convincing, but you keep giving us chance after chance. Why would you do that? I think—and feel free to zap us back to Hell if I'm*" *wrong—that you can't do shit to us."*

"We can't hurt you," said Adeline. "But we can save you."

"Save us?" The bruised ghost's ribs slid back into his chest. *"And why exactly do you think we need saving?"*

"Enough of this garbage," said the dismembered ghost. *"They're trying to keep you talking. We're supposed to kill them, so let's kill them."*

Adeline stood up. "What's the big flaw in your plan?"

"Victims who won't shut the fuck up."

"Think harder."

"You can go ahead and think for me. I'm done with the games."

"Do you want a clue?"

"Sure."

"Exit strategy."

"Okay."

"I'm going to let my eight-year-old daughter tell you what you've overlooked. Naomi, if these ghosts come back as real men, what problem do they still have?"

Naomi shook her head and was silent. Adeline's point would've carried more impact if it was made by a little girl, but she shouldn't have expected Naomi to be able to play along right after watching her father collapse, possibly dead.

"This house is surrounded by cops," said Gina. "You heard the helicopter, right? You might complete your ritual, but you're still screwed. How do you explain being in a house with five dead bodies, two of them children?"

"That is indeed a bit of a pickle. Lucky for you, you'll be dead and don't have to worry about that predicament."

"Then come and get us," said Gina. She looked at the choking ghost. "How many inches of water did you drown in? I bet I could make you drown again in the pool of Boyd's blood."

The ghost didn't seem concerned about that outcome. He ran for Gina, arms out as if planning to wrap his hands around her neck and choke the life out of her for poetic justice.

Gina grabbed one of his hands, swung him around as if doing some sort of strange dance, and then released him. The choking ghost sailed across the basement and then passed through the wall, right where Gina had said his body was buried.

Everybody just stared for a moment.

"*What did you do?*" asked the bruised ghost.

"Returned him to his corpse. He's now rotting inside of his old body, fully conscious but trapped under six feet of dirt. Who's next?"

The bruised ghost and the dismembered ghost exchanged an uneasy glance.

"What, you thought I was bluffing?" asked Gina. "Witches don't bluff. That is Cliff Fletcher's fate: an eternity of being buried alive. You can join him, or you can go back upstairs. I'm done being polite, and I will not ask you again."

"*You bitch.*"

Gina extended her arm toward him. "Come closer and say that again."

The ghosts did not come closer, but they did not return upstairs. Though Adeline wanted to believe that the humans finally had the upper hand, of course Gina *was* bluffing. There was nothing she could do about the other two ghosts. That was all on Boyd. If he still existed.

"I asked you to leave," said Gina.

The ghosts didn't move. Nor did they say anything. They were both staring at the wall where their friend had disappeared.

Adeline looked over at it as well. The cement wall had a small circle of green, as if a patch of mold were rapidly growing upon it. The patch grew and grew, becoming about the size of a lopsided hula-hoop.

She glanced at Gina. It was clear from the woman's expression that she didn't know what was happening.

The patch stopped growing.

A hand emerged.

Then an entire arm. A human arm; not a ghostly one.

And then the tall, bald man crawled out of the hole in the wall, but he wasn't choking any more. He didn't look like a drowned corpse that had been underground for a while. Aside from the dirt, he looked healthy. Strong. Angry.

The black ooze poured down, sealing up the hole.

Gina seemed to be on the verge of panic. Adeline didn't know what the woman had expected, but it definitely wasn't this.

"*Fletcher...?*" asked the bruised ghost.

Fletcher wiped some dirt off his face. His scowl disappeared. He suddenly went from looking pissed off to looking positively joyous.

"Yeah," he said. "I'm back." He took a long, deep breath, and then exhaled slowly, blissfully. "Not what you tried to do to me, is it?" he asked Gina.

Gina didn't answer.

"*Do the same to us,*" the bruised ghost told her. "*Put us back in our bodies. We'll all walk out of here and go our separate ways.*"

"I..."

"*We won't come back for you. Everybody gets to live happily ever after. Do you really think we'd stick around? We'd head straight for the border. You'll never see us again."*

"I can't. His was the only body buried on the property."

Shit. Adeline wished Gina hadn't told him the truth. They could've come up with something else and kept the ghosts at bay a while longer.

"I guess it's back to Plan A, then. Everybody dies."

Fletcher let out a giggle. Coming from a small child, he would've sounded giddy. Coming from a very large adult, he sounded psychotic. He ran toward the stairs.

"Where the fuck are you going?" the bruised ghost demanded.

"I'm getting out of here!"

"Goddamned traitor!"

Fletcher gave him the finger and hurried up the stairs.

Adeline couldn't do anything for Boyd right now. But if Fletcher was flesh and blood, maybe she could stop him. The best scenario would be one in which he opened the front door and perished in a hail of police gunfire. Adeline would not try to prevent him from leaving. However, since nobody actually seemed to completely understand how any of this stuff worked, she needed to make sure Fletcher did not pose a threat if it turned out that he was still trapped in the house with the rest of them.

She didn't want to bring Paige and Naomi upstairs into possible danger, but she also couldn't leave them down here with two ghosts. She tugged on their hands. "Let's go!" she said, running up the stairs after the psychopath.

CHAPTER TWENTY-SIX

*B*oyd's teeth floated in the air around his head, bloody roots forming words he couldn't read. His blood was boiling; he could feel it, hear it, and see the steam coming through his pores. Somehow he was simultaneously falling endlessly and dangling from a giant rusty meat hook.

His intestines spewed out of his belly. They didn't stop. Nobody had this many intestines, but they just kept pouring out and pouring out and pouring out and pouring out...

Finally the last length of bowel came out, taking his spinal column with it. Boyd folded in half. The rest of his bones disappeared (they didn't break through the skin like Maddox's did, they just disappeared, as if they'd never grown inside of him) and he collapsed into a pile of muck.

The muck sprouted squid-like tentacles. Or were they like the tentacles of an octopus? Boyd wasn't sure. He also wasn't sure why he cared about which mollusk the tentacles resembled, considering that the process of sprouting them was so unbearably painful that he shouldn't have been able to think of anything else. He would have shrieked, but piles of muck didn't shriek, even as tentacles sprouted from them.

Then he was back to normal.

Then he had screaming mouths all over his body.

Then the screaming mouths began to vomit up a putrid yellow-brown substance with beaks and feathers in it. The substance burned like gasoline set aflame. Or maybe it just burned like fire. Boyd wasn't sure.

When they were finished vomiting, the mouths popped out on stalks, twisted around, and began to devour Boyd's body. Each mouth had glistening fangs and they had no problem ripping out a generous hunk of meat with each bite, so the process of turning him into a skeleton was completed with relative haste.

Being a skeleton hurt like fuck.

Boyd was glad he didn't have to see himself as a skeleton, but then a giant shimmering lake appeared in the air before him (sideways) so he could see his reflection in an image fifty feet high. No, sixty feet high. No, seventy feet high. No, a million feet high.

His flesh grew back. Boyd didn't know why that would hurt so fucking much, but it did.

He had all of his flesh again, but it wasn't in the right places. At least half of it was on his head, which now flopped backwards from the weight. He couldn't breathe. Maybe he was about to die.

Ha ha ha ha ha ha ha ha ha. No way would this place let him die. He was insane for even thinking such a thing for the fifth of a second that he'd thought it. No death for him! Oh, no! Boyd Gardner was going to get the full Hell experience, even if it wasn't really Hell. Did that mean there wasn't a Hell, or did it mean there was a Hell and he just wasn't there?

He supposed it didn't matter.

No. It mattered a lot.

Did it?

No. It didn't matter at all. He was where he was. Hell, not Hell, all that really mattered was that his body hurt so much that he was surprised he could even think.

The flesh that was making his head too heavy for his neck to hold began to squirm around to the rest of his body like tiny little skin worms.

When his flesh was back to being in the right spot, his jaw exploded again. It was no less horrific the second time. Or was this the third? It was difficult to keep track.

Why was he here again?

There had to be a reason.

Punishment for a life lived poorly?

That didn't seem right. He'd tried to be a good person. He'd never cheated on his wife and always made time for his daughters and was kind to animals and...

Wait, did it count as being kind to animals if he wasn't a vegan? He ate meat. He ate a lot of meat. Was he in Hell because of all those hamburgers?

He vowed to never eat another burger.

Didn't work. He was still in Hell.

He vowed to never drink another glass of milk.

Didn't work. He was still in Hell.

Was he out of Hell now, or was he still in Hell buried up to his neck with scorpions crawling all over his face? He thought it was the latter.

Boyd...

Who was that?

Boyd...

It sounded like him.

It is you.

Oh, good.

You crossed over.

I knew that.

You have to save your family.

Bring me back and I will.

No.

Then fuck you.

You have a job to do.

Like what?

Find the men who are terrorizing your family. They're still here. Find them and kill them.

Kill them? Isn't that the kind of thing that sends people to Hell in the first place?

Find them. Kill them. You can do it if you regain your sanity.

Regain my sanity? I thought my sanity was doing pretty well, all things considered. Oh, look, my hand is a snake.

Find them. Kill them.

Ooooh, watch it slither. I hope I'm not poisonous.

Find them. Kill—

Kill them, I've got it. Can I wait for my skin to stop peeling off like a banana or is sand already running through the hourglass? Have you ever seen what the back of your skin looks like? Not pretty. I wish I didn't know but it's too late now.

Find them. Kill them.

Enough with the mantra. I've got it! Find 'em and kill 'em. At some point you just have to assume that your message has been received instead of repeating it a zillion times. People don't like redundancy.

Who am I doing this for again?

Yeah, yeah, wife and daughters, I know that part, but

I'm foggy on the specifics. Adeline, right? She's one of them. Page? Paige? Paige, yes, and she's the older daughter. Naomi. Is Naomi the wife or the younger daughter? I sure hope I get this right. I can't even imagine how awkward it's going to be for everyone if I get this wrong.

Adeline, wife. Paige, older daughter. Naomi, younger daughter. Gordon, dead pet tarantula. That's all of them. I know my family. Ha! Whoever said I was insane can suck it.

Adeline. Paige. Naomi.

Boyd instantly realized why he was here. He'd sacrificed himself, or at least put himself at very serious risk of sacrificing himself, so he could stop the home invaders.

He screamed in agony. The pain was a lot worse now than it had been when he'd lost his mind, but he'd fight through it.

He had to focus.

Right now he was on a raft made out of severed arms in the middle of a dark red ocean. There were a thousand shark fins circling the raft. But none of this was real. Or, if it was real, it was a flexible reality.

Maybe it was like lucid dreaming. Not that he'd ever had a lucid dream, but he'd read about them. If he could control his environment, he could find the men. And he'd have the element of surprise; they wouldn't be expecting him to have joined them in Hell.

His throat split open.

It wasn't real.

Or at least it wasn't permanent.

He ignored the blood as it gushed out, more blood than a hundred bodies could hold, blood with images of withered faces.

The blood stopped. Froze like a waterfall in the middle of winter. Boyd's neck was frozen to it. More skin tore off his neck as he yanked away, as if his neck was a tongue stuck to a frosty metal pole.

The blood waterfall fell into the ocean.

The severed arms began wiggling underneath him.

One of the sharks rose above the surface. Its skin was covered with knots and scars, and its eyes were eerily human.

The shark didn't matter. If it bit him in half, it wouldn't matter. Boyd would move right on to the next horror.

Lucid dreaming. Lucid dreaming.

Where did he want to be?

He was back in school. Standing at the chalkboard. He'd pissed his pants and all of the other kids were pointing and laughing.

No, they were pointing and laughing because he had no penis.

No, they were pointing and laughing because his crotch was spurting blood.

Had he thought about school?

He wasn't sure.

Boyd did have a recurring dream about school embarrassment, but that was about high school, and the math problems currently on the chalkboard were 5+2 and 7-3.

He ignored his classmates and finished writing on the board. He stepped back and looked at what he'd written: *My family is dead.*

"I'm sorry, Boyd," said Ms. Quincy, his second-grade teacher, who was not wearing a shirt. Her sagging breasts leaked spoiled milk that fell to the floor in clumps. "That answer is incorrect."

The other kids laughed at his stupidity.

Boyd wanted to shout at them, tell them to shut the fuck up, tell them that he was a human being who deserved some dignity, but they weren't real kids, they didn't matter, and it was good that his answer was wrong.

It was the best wrong answer he'd ever given.

Now he was in a bedroom. Not his own bedroom. The room was unfamiliar except for one detail, a detail he'd never forget. A poster of a white kitten. He was in Louise's room. His first girlfriend. Her little brother had drawn a mustache and devil horns on the kitten with magic marker, and Louise's father had beat the shit out of him, right in front of Boyd, even though Boyd had only been over there a couple of times and Louise's father shouldn't have been comfortable enough around him to beat his nine-year-old son with a guest in his home.

Louise had left the defaced poster hanging in her room. Boyd thought it was kind of funny. He was sixteen now. He knew that because he'd dated her at sixteen and didn't have a birthday before they broke up. And he knew what had just happened, because Louise was putting her bra back on.

He'd told his friends he'd lost his virginity. He hadn't. Unless it counted if you finished before you even took your jeans off. He'd been so humiliated that he started crying, which obviously made his humiliation a thousand times worse. Louise hadn't offered any consolation, no "it's okay," not even an offer to get him a tissue to clean himself up. She'd been angry. She'd planned an amazing evening for them and he screwed it all up. She'd threatened to tell everybody about his shame, though ultimately she'd only shared it with her best friend, which Boyd knew because Cecilia started grinning whenever she saw him.

If he was in Hell, yeah, this was an appropriate memory to revisit.

"I have a beautiful wife now," Boyd told Louise. "And we've had lots of great sex. Incredible sex. Not quite as much anymore now that we have kids, but I can last as long as I need to."

"What are you talking about?" asked Louise.

Her father walked into the room. "What the hell is going on in here?" he demanded.

This was a false memory. Boyd had managed to sneak out of the house in his wet sticky pants without her parents noticing. He knew it hadn't happened, and he knew it wasn't really happening now. Still, he was ashamed. Mortified.

Louise would tell everyone.

Everybody would know.

His friends would know.

His parents would know.

He couldn't live here anymore.

No. Stop it. This paralyzing shame was fiction. Louise wasn't really here. And even if she was, it didn't matter, she was in his distant past, he was married to Adeline now, he had two beautiful daughters, and an embarrassing experience with teenage sexuality was no longer relevant to his life.

He was so humiliated that he wanted to kill himself.

He was no longer in Louise's room. He was in Paige's room.

She'd stolen a bottle of Adeline's sleeping pills.

This was real. This had happened.

Paige hadn't taken any of them. She'd set them out in a straight line on her desk. When Boyd caught her sitting there with tears flowing down her face she swore she hadn't actually swallowed any of the pills. She just wanted to look at them.

Paige picked up a pill and put it in her mouth.

This part wasn't real.

She took another.

Also not real.

He couldn't stand here and watch his daughter commit suicide. His mind couldn't handle it even if he knew it was illusion. He wasn't that strong.

"Don't do it, honey," he told her.

Paige swept her arm over the desk, knocking all of the pills to the floor. Then she picked up a box cutter (they didn't own a box cutter, not even after the move), extended the blade, and placed it to her wrist.

"Please don't."

She slashed her left wrist. She did it wrong, you were supposed to go up the arm instead of across the wrist, but blood spurted from the wound and Paige clamped her other hand over it, as if realizing the horror of what she'd done.

"I'm sorry, Dad," she said. "I didn't mean to."

Boyd wanted to help her. He couldn't move.

She switched the box cutter to the arm that was slick with blood, and slashed the other wrist. She let the box cutter fall to the floor as she held up both of her arms. Blood flowed, pouring into her hair and onto her nightgown.

The color faded from her face.

Finally the blood stopped.

Paige reached down, picked up the box cutter, and slashed her wrists again.

New blood spurted.

I can't be here anymore. I can't do this. I don't care if I'm supposed to find those men. I can't stand here and watch my daughter kill herself over and over. Please, Gina, make this end. It was a mistake. It was a terrible mistake. Please, please, please, I'm begging you, bring me back.

Gina did not answer.

He didn't want his family to die for real, but how could he be expected to handle this? It was too much to ask. It wasn't fair.

Paige picked up a pair of scissors. She jabbed them into the gash on her wrist, pushing them in so far that the blade emerged from the other side.

"Why can't I die?" she asked. "I'm ugly and hideous and everybody hates me and I just want to die!"

"I don't want to be here," said Boyd.

Paige stabbed the scissors into her neck.

"I don't want to be here. I don't want to be here. I don't want to be here."

"I don't want to be here, either," Paige said, not removing the scissors from her neck. "It's not about you."

She was right.

She was absolutely right.

He could handle this.

Those three assholes had figured out how this place worked. Why couldn't he? He was stronger than them. He had more to live for. He had everything to live for.

Showing Paige trying to kill herself didn't work. It just reminded Boyd of what he had to live for. Nice try, Hell.

Paige yanked the scissors out of her neck. She opened the blades and stuck her lower lip between them.

Do it. It wasn't real.

Paige cackled with laughter as she sliced off her lip. She held her hand under her mouth for a moment then flicked some blood at Boyd.

It wasn't real.

Now everything was burning. He was in a pool of fire. Burning souls screamed all around him. A huge man, three hundred feet tall, stood at the edge of the pool. Red skin. Horns. Pitchfork.

It wasn't real.

Boyd was falling through the sky. His parachute hadn't opened. His heart felt like it was going to explode from panic.

It wasn't real.

Boyd was covered with leeches. They were all over his body, in his hair, on his eyes, in his mouth, in his stomach.

It wasn't real.

It was a sick joke.

Boyd was in a movie theater. Up on the screen, the image being projected was him, lying on the basement floor. He looked dead.

Maddox sat in the front row, transfixed by the movie.

The dismembered ghost, not dismembered and not a ghost, sat next to him, equally rapt by what he was watching on the screen.

Was *this* real?

It felt real.

Boyd was going to interrupt their movie.

CHAPTER TWENTY-SEVEN

*F*letcher grabbed the doorknob. He cried out and Adeline saw him twitch as if being electrocuted, but he didn't let go, even when smoke billowed from his burning hand.

"Wait in the hallway," said Adeline, as Paige and Naomi hurried past her.

Fletcher turned to look at her. His teeth were clenched together in pain and Adeline would've enjoyed seeing his eyeballs explode in their sockets. Instead, he finally let go of the doorknob. Strips of blackened flesh dangled from his hand.

"I wasn't supposed to be trapped in here," he said, sounding so forlorn that somebody hearing him out of context might have felt genuinely sorry for him.

"Well, you are," said Adeline. "Should we work together to get out of this, or should we waste time trying to kill each other?"

Working with this maniac wasn't actually an option. She was just hoping to keep his guard down for a moment while she tried to kill him. She didn't have the luxury of trying to subdue him. He had to die.

"I guess we have to try to kill each other," said Fletcher.

Adeline ran for the cupboard where she kept the pots and pans. Fletcher ran for a drawer. There were several drawers in the kitchen, but somehow the creep was lucky enough to go straight for the one where they kept the knives.

She grabbed a metal saucepan. Fletcher grabbed a butcher knife.

Adeline held the saucepan up in front of her, defensively. He could stab her to death much more easily than she could beat him to death. Yet she had one big offensive advantage: she was a mother protecting her children. You did not fuck with a mother protecting her children if you wanted to live.

Fletcher was bigger, stronger, and scarier, but Adeline knew she could beat him through sheer force of will.

He might not expect her to charge right at him, so that's what she did. If her plan worked perfectly, she'd smack the butcher knife out of his hand, knock him to the floor with a brutal saucepan blow to the forehead, check to make sure Paige and Naomi weren't watching, and then bash the saucepan against his skull until his brain was visible.

She figured he would hold his ground. She didn't anticipate that he'd fling the butcher knife at her.

It got her in the right shoulder. Probably not where he was aiming. The knife went in deep but didn't stick, so it fell to the tile floor with a clatter, to be quickly joined by the saucepan that fell out of her hand as her fingers spasmed.

Fletcher pulled another knife out of the open drawer. He'd already taken their biggest one, but the bread knife was no joke.

Adeline bent down and picked up the saucepan with her left hand. The fingers on her right hand were still twitching but she managed to grab the butcher knife as well. She stood back up and held them like a sword and shield.

The butcher knife dropped out of her hand.

Fletcher chuckled.

His amused reaction was useful because it gave Adeline an extra boost of rage. She ran at him, ready to dodge if he threw the other knife at her.

He didn't throw the knife, nor did he stab her with it.

When she swung the saucepan at his head, though, he blocked it with his free hand. This was, of course, the hand that had just been mangled by the doorknob. Adeline thought she heard some bones shatter above the *clang*.

Credit where it was due: instead of letting out a high-pitched shriek and crumpling to the floor in tears, as any sensible person would have done, Fletcher punched her in the face. He could have stabbed her in the face, since that hand was clutching the knife, but for some reason he chose to punch her instead.

It was one hell of a punch. Adeline spat out one tooth and accidentally swallowed another. She hoped to live long enough to suffer the discomfort of that tooth making its way through her system.

He punched her again, and she crashed into the counter.

"Mommy!" Naomi screamed.

"Stay where you are!" said Adeline, though her words were garbled. Blood was pouring from her mouth again. But she hadn't dropped the saucepan.

Fletcher held up the knife. "Want it in the gut or the neck?" His face was contorted with pain, and Adeline didn't think his heart was really in the taunt.

"Dealer's choice," said Adeline. It was a staggeringly inept comeback, but hopefully the weak attempt at a clever retort made it clear that her spirit wasn't broken.

Fletcher rushed at her. She swung the saucepan at him, aiming for his face. He blocked the swing with the same hand that had taken so much abuse already. Adeline didn't understand why he kept using that hand. Apparently his time in Almost-Hell had made him good at enduring pain.

This time she was certain she'd broken one of his fingers, because his middle digit was now bent backwards over the top of his hand.

Adeline swung once more. Instead of using his broken, swollen, burnt, and leaking hand to block it, Fletcher used the bread knife. Neither of them dropped their weapons, and no additional harm was caused to either of their bodies.

Fletcher stomped on Adeline's foot. In a fight where Adeline had been struck in the shoulder by a butcher knife, this shouldn't have been his most impactful move up to this point. But he was a big guy and it felt like he'd splattered her foot into mush.

This time, her attempt to bash him in the face with the saucepan was pathetic.

He slammed the knife into her shoulder, almost getting her in the same spot as before but missing by about half an inch. When he released his grip on the knife, it remained in place. He wrenched the saucepan out of her hand and smacked her across the face with it.

Adeline didn't think she lost any additional teeth.

At least not until she dropped to the floor, striking the side of her head. Half a molar broke off.

The fight had most definitely not been beaten out of her, but as Fletcher crouched down over her and wrapped his hands around her neck, she wasn't sure that it mattered.

- - -

Boyd slowly walked toward the home invaders, although he supposed that *he* was the invader right now. Nobody else was in the movie theater. Maddox and Heck didn't move as he stepped into the second row. Nor did they seem to notice as he crept up directly behind them.

Could it really be this easy?

The psychos were in two places at once, but maybe their consciousness was only in the real world. If he had a weapon, he could give them each a quick stab in the back of the neck and end this. He didn't see the third one, so if things were going well on the other side, Fletcher might be trapped beneath six feet of dirt right now.

Lucid dreaming. This was like lucid dreaming. In a lucid dream, if he wanted a weapon, he could create one. He wanted a great big shiny axe. One so sharp that it could cleave their skulls in half with one swing.

He was holding a weapon. It didn't appear in his hand; it was simply like he'd been holding it all along.

It wasn't a great big shiny axe. It was a small, rusty hatchet. Boyd ran his finger along the edge of the blade. It was about as sharp as the edge of a silver dollar. So he wouldn't be cleaving any skulls in half with a single blow, but he could sure as hell finish off a couple of comatose moviegoers.

No time to waste. He raised the hatchet above Heck's head, then slammed it down as hard as he could. The blade sunk deep, far deeper than Boyd would have expected, as if it were passing through candle wax instead of bone.

The hatchet popped out of Boyd's hand as Heck stood up.

- - -

"You think it was funny watching me choke?" Fletcher asked, trying to crush her throat. "Did you get a great big laugh out of that? Huh?"

Adeline hadn't expressed any amusement over his ghostly plight. She'd actually found it rather disturbing. But if Fletcher believed that they were all enjoying a merry joke at his expense, there probably wasn't much she could do to convince him otherwise.

She couldn't breathe.

Fletcher's eyes were wide, crazed. You had to be insane to try to strangle somebody when one of your hands was a ruined mess.

She tried to knee him in the groin, but he wasn't positioned correctly. Her punches to his sides were weak and completely ineffectual.

Fletcher pushed down even harder against her neck. Another finger bone snapped. He didn't look like he even cared.

Though Adeline's spirit was still "the angry mother you don't want to fuck with," her body was fading fast.

- - -

Heck left the hatchet imbedded in the back of his head as he turned around to face Boyd. He swiped at Boyd with a taloned hand, slashing across his chest, removing a huge flap of flesh as easily as if it were the skin on a bowl of soup that had been left sitting too long.

The top layer of Boyd's chest dangled from Heck's talons. Heck shook it off his hand.

Boyd didn't even glance down at himself. He didn't want to see what his chest looked like without skin.

Heck grinned. "Oh, that's fucked up."

Now Boyd couldn't help himself. He looked down. Bloody fish heads, at least a dozen of them, protruded from his skinless chest, mouths opening and closing.

Boyd wanted to throw up. But he should embrace this. Welcome the surrealism. Treat it as a sick joke.

He grabbed at one of the heads, intending to pull it out of his chest and pop it into his mouth. He couldn't get a hold of it; it was too slimy. His hand kept slipping off, even when he tried to dig his fingers into one of their mouths.

"What the hell are you doing?" Heck asked.

Boyd clenched his chest muscles, hoping that the fish would fire out of his body like bullets. They didn't.

Heck held up a pair of garden shears. The black metal blades were long enough to slice through an entire oak tree. He pried the blades open. Boyd's feet, which were now literally nailed to the floor, wouldn't move.

Embrace this...

He calmly stood there.

Heck thrust the shears at him, then closed the blades, neatly severing Boyd's head.

His head bounced on the floor of the theater, which was sticky with spilled sodas, buttered popcorn, and candy.

This was going to be difficult to embrace.

- - -

Adeline was getting dizzy from lack of oxygen. She kept trying to struggle but it wasn't doing any good. It might be time to start praying that Boyd, Paige, and Naomi made it out of this without her.

Paige was right there, blurry.

Holding something.

Glass shattered.

Fletcher's grip on Adeline's neck loosened. His face shot into sharp focus, blood trickling down his forehead. Paige held the handle of a broken bottle of olive oil.

She knelt down and jammed the handle into his back.

Adeline pulled herself out from underneath him. Paige hoisted the glass handle, preparing to stab him again.

"No!" said Adeline.

Paige hesitated. "But he—"

"Go back with Naomi."

Paige shook her head. "He was going to kill you."

"I know he was, honey. And I'm going to take care of it. I don't want you to see it or be part of it. Keep your sister safe. It'll be over in a minute."

Adeline tried to stand but couldn't quite do it. Paige helped her up. Fletcher remained on the floor, groaning.

"Go," Adeline said. Her children were going to need every therapist in the world after this was over, but she didn't want to make it even worse. This was a sight that would never leave their mind's eye.

Paige reluctantly returned to the hallway with Naomi.

"Don't watch," said Adeline. "Don't let Naomi watch.

Go in the living room. I'll be right there."

Paige took Naomi's hand and led her out of sight. Adeline opened a cabinet and took out the crockpot. It had been a present from her parents about five years ago. She rarely used it and it was almost one of the possessions that didn't make it from the apartment to the house. This would most definitely not be in the spirit in which their gift was intended.

Fletcher wiped some blood from his scalp. "You don't need to do that," he said.

Adeline slammed the crockpot down upon his skull.

Fletcher's entire body convulsed.

She bashed him a second time. The ceramic inner bowl fell out and broke in half.

Adeline bashed him again with the stainless steel exterior.

His skull was caved in enough that he would not be moving, speaking, or breathing ever again. Adeline didn't want to regress into complete savagery, so she only bashed him twice more, splattering the contents of his cranium all over the thoughtful gift.

The Gardner family had many problems remaining in their lives, but Cliff Fletcher was not one of them.

CHAPTER TWENTY-EIGHT

*E*mbrace this.
Everything was fine.
Ideal, even.

Many people would love to be a severed head. Less responsibility. Nobody telling you to lose weight. No fish heads protruding from your chest. Of course, it was more difficult to see a movie screen, as he was proving to himself right now, but you had to take the bad with the good.

Heck climbed over the seat. The hatchet was still buried in his head. "Not as easy as you thought, huh?" he asked.

Embrace this.

Hell can be fun with the right attitude.

Boyd wanted to say, "I like a challenge," but no words came out. He assumed it was because he no longer had lungs. This was an odd time for the logic of biology to play a role.

He should probably try to acquire a new body.

Now his head was on a new body.

He would've loved for it to be a cartoonishly muscular body, or a dragon's body, or a voluptuous woman's body, or something amusing or powerful like that. Instead, his severed head was attached (with what felt like duct tape) to a body that looked like it was one missed meal away from starving to death. The kind of depleted frame you'd see on a commercial asking you to give generously.

Heck reached back and wrenched the hatchet out of his head. "I don't even need this to cut you in half," said Heck. "I could just use my fingernail."

New body. He needed a new body.

His new body had red, cracked skin that itched so badly that he couldn't stop himself from violently scratching, even as flakes of skin came off. Even as chunks of skin came off. It was a relief to scrape his flesh down to the bone.

New body.

He was covered in pustules. The itching hadn't ceased, though now he felt like he had every sexually transmitted disease with which humanity had ever been afflicted. Pustules on his tongue burst as he ran it over the bubbling roof of his mouth.

New body.

Nope. Didn't work. Same pustule-covered body.

"What did you hope to accomplish here?" asked Heck.

There was too much pus in Boyd's mouth for him to answer.

Embrace this.

Lucid dream.

Sick joke.

He was not in a land of eternal torment. He was in a very dark, very twisted playground. He could do whatever he wanted. He could command a skeleton army. He could ride a black stallion with glowing eyes and breath of fire.

The itching was so maddening that he ran his fingernails all the way down his chest. *Pop. Pop. Pop.*

Heck held out his index finger, middle finger, and thumb, then slammed them into Boyd's face. They sunk all the way to the second knuckle. He pulled them out, leaving holes in Boyd's forehead and the bridge of his nose.

"Not what I meant to do," Heck admitted. "I was going for your eyes. Trying to use you like a bowling ball."

New body.

Nope. Same itchy pustule-ridden one. He'd take literally anything over this, even the severed head on the sticky floor.

Visions of Paige began to float around the movie theater, a hundred bonus screens of content. In one, she was slashing her wrists. In another, she was downing a bottle full of pills. In another, she shoved a revolver into her mouth. Stepped in front of a bus. Draped a noose around her neck. Leapt off a bridge.

"You're losing," said Heck.

New body.

Old body. His real body.

Not his real body. His real body was bleeding to death in his basement. He was in his body the way it looked before the ghosts arrived.

Paige died around him, over and over, and Boyd mentally praised her dedication to the cause and her ingenuity. There she was trying to kill herself with a power drill. How many thirteen-year-old girls would commit suicide with a power drill? Not very damn many. Or maybe in that vision she wasn't trying to kill herself. Maybe she was trying to give herself a lobotomy. If you took a survey of a thousand thirteen-year-old girls and asked them to describe how you went about lobotomizing yourself, maybe two of them would get it right, and the other one would be some fucked-up kid who was planning to lobotomize her enemies.

He was proud of his daughter.

No, he—

Yes, he was. He was the proudest father in the world. Look at the way those globs of brain matter exploded out of the back of her head, creating abstract art on the wall behind her. That was goddamn talent.

Pin a medal on that kid. Use a 1st place trophy to scoop up her brains.

The images disappeared.

Lucid dreaming. Embrace it. Enjoy it. Theme park ride. Carnival. Haunted house—the fun kind.

A whole new set of images appeared. Scary clowns. Clowns beckoning to children. Clowns with knives. Clowns with fangs.

Boyd wasn't scared of clowns. Never had been. He thought their antics were delightfully amusing, just as they intended.

The clowns vanished.

Boyd punched Heck in the face. His fist went all the way through. He slid his hand out then licked the red goop off his fingers, because he was enjoying the ride.

Heck's face reconstructed itself.

Boyd punched him again. He wished he could grab Heck's uvula and dangle it in front of his face but that wasn't working out.

Heck's face reconstructed itself around Boyd's fist. Pulling it free was difficult, though he managed.

Heck swung at him with talons that had sprouted to

six feet long. Boyd ducked out of the way.

No, wait. He hadn't quite ducked out of the way. The top of his head slid off.

New head.

Boyd grabbed a plastic cup from one of the seat's drink holders. He squeezed it, sending a spray of cola-colored carbonated beverage into Heck's face. His face began to sizzle and smoke.

Maddox continued to watch the movie, motionless.

Boyd yanked the screaming Heck by the back of his collar and dragged him over to the wall. Boyd slammed him against it, crushing his head into slime.

Now Heck was on the other side of the theater, back to normal. How was there supposed to be a winner in a fight where they both kept coming back to life?

Perhaps there wasn't. Perhaps he was doomed to keep doing this forever.

No. Lucid dreaming. Roller coaster. Sick joke.

They were on a ship.

Heck looked confused. Surely he was used to the way things worked here, but this change in location appeared to have taken him completely off-guard.

"Don't like water?" Boyd asked.

"You shouldn't have come here."

"The ship?"

"*Here*. Hell."

"I'm told it's not quite Hell."

"You've made the stupidest mistake anybody has ever made. I mean ever. In the history of humanity. You're going to be stuck here forever, suffering every second of every day until the end of the universe, and I'm going to return to your basement to kill your wife, kill your daughters, and then be set free. Maybe I'll hunt down your parents. Your friends."

"I don't think you know how to get back."

"I'll figure it out. We figured it out the first time."

"The first time you weren't distracted by me killing you again and again."

Heck smiled. "Maybe Hell won't be so bad if I get to kill you on an infinite loop. That's more like Heaven, huh?"

"Who do you think can kill each other the most times?"

"Should we keep score?"

"No," said Boyd. "Trying to kill you was a blunder on my part. You can't die here. I was wasting my time with that. I just need you to not cross over again."

Lucid dreaming.

Thrill ride.

Sick joke.

What could be a crueler punchline than sending Heck to the permanent state of drowning Fletcher had endured?

Suddenly Heck's body, everything but his head, turned to iron. His smile faltered.

The wood beneath him began to crack.

"It's not..." he began, but was unable to finish his sentence before he broke through the bottom of the ship and plunged into the sea.

Boyd peered through the hole. The water was too dark to see Heck sinking, so he just had to imagine it. How long would it take him to reach the bottom? Did a sea in Hell even have a bottom?

Boyd wasn't the type of person to gloat, and quite honestly, condemning somebody to an eternity of suffocation was not something he should celebrate even if the person was a piece of crap who'd tried to hurt his family. He needed to get back and seal Maddox's fate.

He was back in the movie theater. This was easy.

His body was still on the screen.

Some drops of blood pattered onto the basement floor next to it.

That was weird. What was happening?

Boyd opened his eyes. The agony of being in Hell was replaced by his former pain of all of the injuries he'd inflicted in the real world.

More blood drops fell to the floor.

Maddox held Gina tightly. His broken ribs were deep in her chest.

He shoved her away and she collapsed, the front of her body a ghastly mess.

"*Oh, I'm sorry,*" said Maddox to Boyd. "*Did I cut your little field trip short?*"

CHAPTER TWENTY-NINE

"*N*ot a lot you can do without your guide, is there?*" asked Maddox. His ribcage retracted back into his chest. "*Well, you can watch that bitch die. I think she's got a few more seconds left in her.*"

Boyd tried to get up but didn't have the strength. Ironically, he'd been better off in Hell.

"*Lucky for you, you're hurt too bad for me to drag you around to watch your wife and kids die. I'd bring them down here and kill them in front of you, but I'm not sure you'll last that long, and I'm ready to wrap this shit up.*"

- - -

The kitchen door burst open. Adeline spun toward the cops (or were they FBI?) who held the battering ram.

The black ooze poured down. The men, possibly having learned from the other cop's tragic fate, were not standing in the doorway. Within seconds, the doorway was sealed with the ooze, and Adeline's momentary hope that beating Fletcher to death had solved their problem was dashed.

Nobody from the outside would be saving them. Fine. They didn't need the police, FBI, military, or whatever. They had a witch. Adeline was confident that she'd return to the basement to discover that Boyd had dealt with the other two ghosts, and they could finally get out of this house and go back to that amazing burger place for dinner.

"Stay up here unless I call you," Adeline told the girls. Since Paige had saved her life, having them stay upstairs might not be the best decision from a tactical standpoint, but Adeline couldn't just turn off her desire to keep her children out of danger.

She looked down the stairs and gasped.

Gina lay on the floor, covered in blood. Boyd was also on the floor, almost where she'd left him, now awake. The bruised ghost stood between them. It noticed Adeline at the top of the stairs and gave her a playful wave.

"C'mon down and join us."

"Your friend is dead. I killed him."

"Can you prove it?"

"Yes."

"I trust you. No need for you to cut off his head or anything. Fletcher was an okay guy, but he had no problem running out on us, so if you killed him, kudos. I hope it was gross."

"It was."

"Good. You can't escape the house until my ritual is complete, and my ritual isn't complete until you're dead, so by that logic, you can never escape the house. So you can come down here and just offer your throat to me to get it over with, or I can chase you around until you pass out. Your call."

Gina wasn't dead.

Adeline wasn't sure how she knew this. The woman

looked dead. She was unquestionably dying. But though the illumination from the kitchen was enough to show off her grisly wounds, it wasn't sufficient to tell if she was breathing or not.

Gina definitely wasn't dead yet. She wasn't quite *talking* to Adeline—it wasn't as if she could hear Gina's voice in her mind—but she understood the message she was conveying as if it were her own thoughts. If Gina hadn't told them about how she "puppeteered" the home invaders, Adeline might have believed that these *were* her own thoughts.

Maddox didn't realize that he'd already won.

Murdering Adeline, Boyd, Paige, and Naomi would indeed complete the ritual. They lived in the home, and it was their energy the ghosts had used to cross back over. When the last of them lay dead, Maddox would return to his human form and be able to escape this prison.

But so would killing Gina.

Was that good? If Maddox didn't have to kill them to get what he wanted, did that mean their nightmare was almost over?

Adeline was amused by the question. Well, no, it wasn't her amusement, even though it felt that way. She was feeling Gina's sense of amusement like it was her own.

No. Their nightmare was only beginning.

Maddox could get out of the house. They couldn't.

They'd be trapped inside with no way to ever escape.

They'd starve to death.

They'd have to decide whether to eat the dead to prolong their lives for a few extra days.

Couldn't she just kill Maddox? Bash him to death with the same crockpot that had destroyed Fletcher?

Sorry, no, that would be lovely, but that's not the way it would work. Maddox didn't have to walk out the door. He could go anywhere he wanted. Moments after Gina died, he'd be relaxing on a Caribbean beach, sipping a refreshing cocktail out of a pineapple and chuckling about the slow, miserable deaths of the Gardner family.

Maddox didn't know he'd won.

That was it. That was the way to beat him.

Adeline walked down the stairs, moving slowly but not too slowly. She needed to time this perfectly, and yet she didn't know exactly when Gina would perish.

"I can't die like that," Adeline told Maddox. "If there's no happy ending, just kill me now. If you promise to make it quick I won't struggle."

"*I like the struggle.*"

"Paige! Naomi! Come down here!" If Adeline was going to play the role of somebody who'd completely given up, she had to believably sell it. She wouldn't let Maddox kill her and just leave her daughters upstairs to be hunted.

Adeline reached the bottom of the stairs.

Gina was holding on. She was purposely clinging to life. Did she know what Adeline was thinking?

"Swear to me you'll make it quick," said Adeline.

"*All right,*" said Maddox. "*I'll make it relatively painless for the youngsters. You and your hubby...well, I'd like you to suffer a little.*"

"That's not good enough."

"*Take it or leave it.*"

Adeline lifted her arms, showing that she meant him no harm. "I'm not going to resist. Give me one of your special hugs."

She walked toward him.

"I love you, Boyd," she said.

"Don't do this," Boyd told her. He sounded heartsick and quite clearly was not playing along. "There has to be another way."

"There isn't. It's over for us. Why drag it out?"

She stopped. The timing was off.

"*Getting scared?*" asked Maddox.

Gina was ready to let go. She wasn't afraid to die.

Adeline walked over to Maddox. She held her arms out for the embrace.

Maddox's jagged ribs burst out of his chest.

"*Actually, I'll make it even quicker,*" he told her. Sharp bones ripped through each of his arms. "*Give Daddy a great big hug.*"

Gina died.

Maddox's body changed. The bruises faded. His skin lost its ghostly transparency and became flesh again. He looked surprised, and then elated, almost orgasmic as he realized what was happening.

He'd completed the ritual.

He'd crossed back over.

He was human again.

And his ribcage was on the outside of his chest.

He clutched at the bones as his blood spilled, as if trying to shove them back in. His eyes went wide with panic. He looked at Adeline and opened his mouth, trying to say something that was surely a variation on "*You fucking bitch,*" but he wasn't able to articulate it before he fell over.

Adeline could finish him off pretty easily, deliver the final blow, but no, it was perfectly fine to let him bleed to death.

"Did you really kill Fletcher?" Boyd asked.

"Yes."

"I trapped Heck at the bottom of a sea in Hell."

"Excellent."

"When Maddox bleeds out, I think that's it."

"I think you're right."

They watched Maddox for a few moments. His eyes glazed over and he stopped breathing.

"Let's get out of this place," said Adeline, helping Boyd to his feet. "Please don't die when we're this close to freedom."

"I think I've got a couple of hours left in me."

Adeline gave him a kiss.

Paige and Naomi were at the top of the stairs. "Paige, I may need you to help me," said Adeline.

"Are they all dead?"

"Yes, honey."

"Well, no, one of them is trapped under the sea," said Boyd. "He got a raw deal. But they won't be hurting us anymore."

Adeline stepped onto the first stair. Her foot broke through. The wood had rotted.

Paige tentatively pressed her foot against the top step. "I don't think this will hold us."

"That's fine. Stay up there. We'll figure it out."

The stairs were all changing color. A stair in the middle began bowing in the center, as if it was turning to clay. Adeline looked up and saw the ceiling beginning to bow as well.

"Get someplace safe!" she shouted. "Hurry!"

Paige and Naomi ran off.

A board dropped from the ceiling, landing corner-first on Maddox's dead face. More boards followed.

Adeline hated leaving Gina. It felt disrespectful to let a

house collapse upon somebody who'd sacrificed herself for them, but they had to find a secure place to hide.

Brownish black liquid began to leak between the boards.

Where could they hide if the whole house came down? It wasn't like there was a refrigerator down here where they could just shut themselves inside and hope for the best.

A long, thick board landed right in front of them. But it splattered a bit upon impact.

A dribble of liquid hit Adeline's head and she screamed.

There was no burning sensation. Just wetness. This wasn't like the ooze that had killed the police officer.

Boards slapped against the basement floor like wet cardboard. The smell was so unspeakably vile that it overwhelmed any sense of victory Adeline might be feeling.

A huge piece of the ceiling collapsed, and the dining room table fell from above with it. A second later, the sofa came crashing down to the floor, with both Paige and Naomi on it.

A chunk of mostly liquid wood struck Boyd's head.

The ping-pong table was turning to goo.

The metal shelves were turning to rust.

The sofa was rotting beneath Paige and Naomi. They hurriedly got off of it, as shaken as one might naturally expect young girls to be when they'd ridden a sofa that dropped through the floor into the basement.

The oven fell into the basement, shattering into rust-colored particles, followed by the refrigerator and the kitchen sink.

Everything was liquefying so quickly now that there

wasn't anything they could do to escape it. Adeline, Boyd, Paige, and Naomi held each other as reeking slop poured down upon them.

Within a minute, it was up to their waists and rising.

Holy shit—they were going to drown in it!

Boyd was in no condition to have a child on his shoulders, so Adeline boosted Naomi onto her back. The slime was rising to their chests and it was hard to move around in it, with swimming being impossible for sure. The top of the house was almost gone.

And finally it was over.

Adeline and Paige were up to their necks, but there was nothing left to rot and add to their makeshift swimming pool. The four of them were just standing in black muck in a great big hole in the ground.

A helicopter flew overhead.

As they slowly made their way to the edge, cops began to peer into the hole, along with firefighters and military personnel. Somebody with a megaphone told civilians to keep back.

Two men in HAZMAT suits lowered a thick rope into the hole. They pulled Naomi out, then Paige. Boyd urged Adeline to go next, and though he needed medical attention more quickly than she did, she decided to let him have his pride.

As she emerged from the hole, she saw police cars, fire trucks, news vans, and literally hundreds of onlookers, all of whom seemed to have their cell phones out and recording.

This was not going to be easy to explain.

EPILOGUE

They spent several days in quarantine. Being neck-deep in pure rot was not ideal for people covered with wounds, but they were under the care of an excellent medical team that kept their cuts and gashes from getting infected.

Since they had an eight-year-old who couldn't credibly lie about sneaking a Twinkie out of the cupboard, they decided to go with most of the truth. Considering that hundreds of people had watched their house basically melt into black ooze (not counting the millions who watched it online) they didn't feel ridiculous sharing the more outlandish parts of their adventure.

Boyd decided not to talk about the place that wasn't quite Hell, instead saying that he'd blacked out and didn't remember it. Despite everything else that happened, that part felt like it might land him in a sanitarium.

They tried to stay out of the public eye as much as possible. Somehow they'd managed to get through this without Paige and Naomi going completely catatonic, and now it was important to return them to as much of a normal life as was possible. Oh, that didn't mean Boyd and Adeline wouldn't consider book deals, a TV series, or any of the other assorted rewards of infamy, but they wanted to keep things low-key for a while. Take the time to heal mentally and physically. Figure out their future beyond a time when at least one of them woke up screaming every night.

- - -

Several months later, they lived in a modest home where Paige and Naomi still had their own rooms, though they usually slept in the same room at night.

They'd had a delicious pizza, with cinnamon sticks for dessert, and it was time to break out the board games (Naomi got to pick tonight) when the doorbell rang.

Four men stood on the front porch when Boyd answered.

"Hello, Mr. Gardner," said the one in the middle. He looked about sixty, with a neatly trimmed gray beard and thick eyebrows.

"May I help you?"

"We're here for a business opportunity."

"Sorry," said Boyd. "All of that goes through my agent. I can give you his card."

The man pointed a revolver at Boyd's face. "I think we can discuss this now. Please step into your home and remain quiet."

Boyd stepped back into his living room. The four men followed, closing the door behind them. The man with the gun nodded, and the other three men walked past Boyd.

"If you touch them, I'll—"

"I asked you not to speak," said the man. "You made

it through a lot. It would be a shame to get shot in the face after all that."

The men were quick and efficient. After the sounds of a brief struggle, they returned to the living room with Adeline, Paige, and Naomi, each with black hoods over their heads. The men forced them to their knees.

"I'm not going to stretch this out too long," said the man with the gun. "We're here to execute your wife and daughters, and then you. Please know that it isn't your fault. You simply rented the wrong house."

"You're making a mistake," said Boyd.

"We hired some men to commit a truly heinous act. You are very familiar with these three men. I don't need to name them, right?"

"I know who you're talking about."

"They did their job and I should have had a lot of power. You would not approve of how I wished to use this power. People like you can be very judgmental."

"You don't know me."

"I know enough about you. I've had plenty of time to do my research while we waited for this opportunity. You're a popular guy, Mr. Gardner."

"Very popular. So maybe you shouldn't murder me and my family."

"You're also extremely familiar with a woman named Gina, who took matters into her own hands and spoiled things for me. I can't blame her for being angry about her sister. I'd do the same thing in her position."

"Gina's dead now."

"I know that, obviously. If I'd known Gina was responsible, I could have used her blood to regain what she took from me, but sadly, she died in your home. However, I believe that you, your wife, and your daughters can serve the same purpose. It's an ugly cycle of death. I wish there was another way."

"You need to leave," said Boyd.

"Not quite yet."

"No, now. You need to take your goons and leave my house immediately."

The man didn't quite smile. "I feel that you don't understand how little power you have to intimidate me."

"I'm not trying to intimidate you. I'm trying to warn you."

"About what?"

"I've been to Hell. Well, close enough."

"Have you?"

"Let me tell you something about paying a visit to Hell. Something that wasn't part of the warning I was given. There are side effects. You bring some of it back with you. It gives you horrible, terrifying power. That's something I have to live with for the rest of my life. I don't want to abuse it. Let me rephrase that: I'll *never* abuse it. But don't think for one second that I won't do everything I can to protect my family. So let me ask you one more time to leave my home."

The man looked into Boyd's eyes as if trying to decide if he was telling the truth. Finally, he lowered the gun.

"I apologize for disturbing you. We'll be going now."

"I think you'll come back. And I can't let that happen."

One of the men clutched at his face as blood spewed from his nostrils, mouth, and eyes. The other two men did the same. The blood burnt their flesh as it poured down their faces, as if it had come from a boiling cauldron.

The first man tried to raise his gun again, but blood

shot from his arm in several different places, like the limb had become a leaky pipe.

"Leave the hoods on," said Boyd to his family. "Don't take them off."

Soon all four of the men were spraying blood from random places on their body, blood that hissed as it struck the floor.

It didn't take them long to die.

Boyd held his hand to his mouth until the urge to vomit was gone. He prayed he'd never have to do this again.

"Everything's fine," he said. "All of you keep the hoods on. I'll lead you to the other room. You don't need to see this."

"I'm scared," said Naomi.

"Don't be scared," Boyd told her. "Everything is going to be okay, I promise you. Daddy just has to get rid of some bodies."

- The End -

OTHER BOOKS BY JEFF STRAND

Everything Has Teeth. A third collection of short tales of horror and macabre comedy.

An Apocalypse of Our Own. Can the Friend Zone survive the end of the world?

Stranger Things Have Happened. Teenager Marcus Millian III is determined to be one of the greatest magicians who ever lived. Can he make a shark disappear from a tank?

Cyclops Road. When newly widowed Evan Portin gives a woman named Harriett a ride out of town, she says she's on a cross-country journey to slay a Cyclops. Is she crazy, or...?

Blister. While on vacation, cartoonist Jason Tray meets the town legend, a hideously disfigured woman who lives in a shed.

The Greatest Zombie Movie Ever. Three best friends with more passion than talent try to make the ultimate zombie epic.

Kumquat. A road trip comedy about TV, hot dogs, death, and obscure fruit.

Facial. Carlton just found a dead lion in his basement. This is the normal part of the story.

I Have a Bad Feeling About This. Geeky, non-athletic Henry Lambert is sent to survival camp, which is bad enough *before* the trio of murderous thugs show up.

Pressure. What if your best friend was a killer...and he wanted you to be just like him? Bram Stoker Award nominee for Best Novel.

Dweller. The lifetime story of a boy and his monster. Bram Stoker Award nominee for Best Novel.

A Bad Day For Voodoo. A young adult horror/comedy about why sticking pins in a voodoo doll of your history teacher isn't always the best idea. Bram Stoker Award nominee for Best Young Adult Novel.

Dead Clown Barbecue. A collection of demented stories about severed noses, ventriloquist dummies, giant-sized vampires, sibling stabbings, and lots of other messed-up stuff.

Dead Clown Barbecue Expansion Pack. A few more stories for those who couldn't get enough.

Wolf Hunt. Two thugs for hire. One beautiful woman. And one vicious frickin' werewolf.

Wolf Hunt 2. New wolf. Same George and Lou.

The Sinister Mr. Corpse. The feel-good zombie novel of the year.

Benjamin's Parasite. A rather disgusting action/horror/comedy about why getting infected with a ghastly parasite is unpleasant.

Kutter. A serial killer finds a Boston terrier, and it might just make him into a better person.

Faint of Heart. To get her kidnapped husband back, Melody has to relive her husband's nightmarish weekend, step-by-step...and survive.

Mandibles. Giant killer ants wreaking havoc in the big city!

Graverobbers Wanted (No Experience Necessary). First in the Andrew Mayhem series.

Single White Psychopath Seeks Same. Second in the Andrew Mayhem series.

Casket For Sale (Only Used Once). Third in the Andrew Mayhem series.

Lost Homicidal Maniac (Answers to "Shirley"). Fourth in the Andrew Mayhem series.

Suckers (with JA Konrath). Andrew Mayhem meets Harry McGlade. Which one will prove to be more incompetent?

Gleefully Macabre Tales. A collection of thirty-two

demented tales. Bram Stoker Award nominee for Best Collection.

The Severed Nose. What would you do if you came home one evening and found a severed nose lying on a plate on your dining room table?

Disposal. Frank, a self-proclaimed scumbag, is hired to murder an old man...but the old bastard just won't DIE!!!

Elrod McBugle on the Loose. A comedy for kids (and adults who were warped as kids).

Out of Whack. A coming-of-age comedy about love, friendship, and the realization that trying to yank somebody's panties off in a passionate manner can only lead to wedgies.

How to Rescue a Dead Princess. A ridiculous spoof of fantasy novels. Lots and lots and lots of jokes, but I'm willing to admit that it perhaps tries a bit too hard.

The Haunted Forest Tour (with Jim Moore). The greatest theme park attraction in the world! Take a completely safe ride through an actual haunted forest! Just hope that your tram doesn't break down, because this forest is PACKED with monsters...

Draculas (with JA Konrath, Blake Crouch, and F. Paul Wilson). An outbreak of feral vampires in a secluded hospital. This one isn't much like *Twilight.*

For information on all of these books, visit Jeff Strand's more-or-

less official website at http://www.jeffstrand.com

Subscribe to Jeff Strand's free monthly newsletter at http://eepurl.com/bpv5br

Printed in Great Britain
by Amazon

67350630R00177